EXACTING CLAM No. 5 — Summer 2022

I0667973

CONTENTS

Front cover: "Summer" by Kathleen Nicholls

Interior art by John Patrick Higgins & Zdeněk Macháček/Unsplash

© 2022 Sagging Meniscus Press
All Rights Reserved

ISBN: 978-1-952386-43-5

Exacting Clam is a quarterly publication from Sagging Meniscus.

Senior Editors: Aaron Anstett, Jesi Bender, Jeff Chon, Elizabeth Cooperman, Tyler C. Gore, Charles Holdefer, Kurt Luchs, M.J. Nicholls, Doug Nufer, Thomas Walton

Executive Editor: Guillermo Stitch

Publisher: Jacob Smullyan

exactingclam.com

M.J. NICHOLLS

Epitext Is Your Enemy

Zacharia Hoss—

You wrote to me on pre-launch palpitations ahead of the event for your "post-orbital ravioli western" *Dead Liquor Store*. My thoughts on the matter flow below in a bloat of yummy graphemes.

Zacharia, the act of authoring is a mysterious process—a hy-   per-holy consecration be-   tween the imagination and   the page. There are no suitable terms to explain this almighty transfer from brain to book, my biblically labelled non-friend, so crudely wielded religious imagery will have to suffice. As an author, you must protect this unknowable, super-sacred sanctitic process, and the shimmering halos of heavenly prose that result (assuming you have any talent, of course, which your attached excerpt suggests you may), with your every feeble sinew.

If you've ever slobbered your way through several yonks of literary studies, you may have heard of French notioneer Gérard Genette's coinage *paratext*—a termic pater for texts orbiting the text itself, spawning the children *peritext* (titles, notes, prefaces) and *epitext* (blurbs, reviews, interviews). Genette labels these paratexts "a zone between text and off-text [. . .] at the service of a better reception of the text." On read-

ing this lone line, I prod his scruffy theory out to sea on a schooner of contempt.

The epitext is your enemy. Everything in the epitextual realm seeks to undermine the potency of that unknowable process of authoring I mentioned mere minims ago by forcing the wibbling bag of frailty and chin-stroking responsible for the novel (you) into sparsely occupied rooms where you are invited to piss upon this process by publicly mangling your words, turning the focus away from the merits of their magic to the humiliating reality of your bodily flumps—your stammer, your accent, your hideousness—anything to skew the viewer to the prospect that your prose probably resembles this inadequate self. Or—that sentence in shorter form—they will equate your many bodily bloopers with the calibre of your prose. The two have no connection, my zeddy correspondent, and I will embark upon explainish noises below.

My first book (the offensively under-reviewed dystopian literary satire *The House of Writers*) was "launched" (for more on this verbicide see my response to Carl Totale) in 2016 in a vegan caff frequented by quondam humanities students and molesters of earnestness unwowed in the presence of high literary voltage—everyday Facebook selfists who love nibbling vegan kibble in the vicinity of high literary voltage while completely shunning the reading, the author, and the book—swatting away any offers of taking a cursory glance at the printed object itself—while blathering about their upcoming retreats to corporate internships as they end their artistic phase and enter their lifespans of one book a year.

To avoid the embarrassment of speaking my words in a hesitant and shaky manner to roomful of indifferent falafel-munchers, I hired a voice actor to read selected slices of illustratively twinkly prose, and plopped myself in tatty chair to sip prosecco and chuckle heartily to myself at my own risibility. I was back in my teenage bedroom, making myself chuckle to pass the lonely Sunday mornings with violent cartoons and forays into comic listicles before listicles were a thing. Here, at the apex of my literary ambitions, I sat semi-drunk in a chair, watching a paid actor read my own prose back to me, entirely for my own amusement. This reaffirmed my view that the writer writes for himself, and any audience for his work is utterly accidental. In that particular room, the book I wrote for my own amusement was being launched entirely for my own amusement for the intended audience of one—me—and as much as my invited friends surrendered smirks of solidarity at the notion of me ever trying my hand at "public authorship"—there was no denying the Onan of this-ism.

So, Mr. Hoss, for me, there is no higher reward for the prose writer than the way the prose the prose writer has written pirouettes across the prosey proseface of their prosily prosèd pages. The only plea-sure in authorship resides in that collision of word upon word, the surf of syllables ten-fiving across the page with the fleet boardwork of a seasoned sea-dude, and the magisterial power in corralling the imagination into utterly sublime sentences of epic sensuality . . . possessing a temporary form of mastery over something in a world utterly untameable and unlovable.

Turning up to literary events, surrounded by your well-intentioned, envious, or embarrassed peers, less than 1% of whom may end up actually reading (some) of your words, is nothing less than a ritual humiliation for an author. If you wish to despoil your creations, Mr. Hoss, if you wish to subject your little ripples of lexical magic to acres of hurt, the worst thing you can do is to show yourself in public and feed your brilliance to the ravenous vampires of epitext. The text has its place on the page and must remain there.

Hold firm—

M.J.

TRIOS

Trios are not to be confused with ceviche (suhVEEchay). Trios are inedible. Trios consist,
among other features, of targets. (Alternately, Trios consist
of, among other features, targets.)

Refrigerate. Reduce scallops to tears, with a thin slice of weevil. Include agencies,
soviets, covens, jirgas and a peshmerga or two. They do what they can,
thinking it's never enough.

The plumb bob's devotion. Ah, such terrain! It is here
(not just anywhere), a perfect table
setting.

One notes chaos skulking amidst a necessary
obscurity. Also kanakas abusing
ukuleles.

Scented bubbles. White tiles like petite vault doors
enclosing toy pandas, dream
ing.

Perfection pierced with cocktail umbrellas, had stupid gas a sentient thing been,
in the foreground, pantry
moths.

Plenty of which to carry us when? To cakewalking back with Buonaparte's horde
like bloated scarabs in tatty duds? Utah! Wetah!
Trios!

Kitsch inspiring zits. Wound-oozy martyrs approve. To be synchronous with plumbing's
captive fluids, looks of anticipation, clouds doing what clouds do,
thanks to you, comrade sky.

X endures, Y not so much. What next wonders the plug snug in its jug
and so do you. Have we climbed the wrong ziggurat?
Ducking's an option.

Tree surgeon in error lynched. Good luck deposits where Mother Lode lodges.
I shall too soon to achievements aspire, crafting illusions
of moist effusions.

When off a roof a walkabout stumbles, nasals oboe dirge morose,
cello, tuba, trombone euphonious. It's in the pavement
dissonance dwells.

Aflame the ballroom at which one arrives for modish bamboula,
opaque with smoke, spattered Maz
ola.

At ante-matter one fusses and fumbles, bigger even than
phantom conundrums. Is this even
possible?

Question accountancy. Investigative poetry demands it. Suns set,
onslaughts befall. Your years differ from mine,
beginning at the orphanage.

Heard the one about the Senegalese merchant?
Seems his camels are strangers.
Strange camels.

Above all else (hands to breast), Mother of God! They say I shall hurt me,
yes, they do say it. The deed will remain
in the family aisle.

Why does Respighi gnaw his fedora? One declines to water seedlings.
The future lies. Rifts in Ancient
Airs and Dances.

As any sniper knows, success is the carom's best friend. How less than fulfilling
to aspire to the heavens imagined through a ceiling that falls on
one's face. Moon. Crickets. Stars.

In discarding oneself one could, I suppose, aim for the trash and achieve thereby,
of courtesy and comity, a comely
simultaneity.

Kit Carson's dead. Because we have our wisdom teeth
we understand that these things
happen.

I seem the buffoon in Donald Duck pumps? Is it, again, the vision thing? Is it bad judgment,
the hours spent quacking, dreaming duck dreams, seeing the stars
as eggs to be cracked?

This leg I'm on might be my last. It's also tough on elderly voles. How to queue?
By size? By diploma? As little drips maelstroms begin, no more alarming
than ziti al dente.

Guillaume Apollinaire, Guillaume de Machaut, Billy the Kid,
William B. Williams, utility
bill.

Colleen, my colleen, o'demeanor kayacky, your features I bathe in dancing confetti,
the kind one dumps from high office
windows.

Osaka noodles! Hai! Banzai! So why does a lady
have a roach on her
libido?

Knee-deep in mud. How to upgrade:
Shop for an arm
oire.

Assemble the family. Hand out cotton swabs. Explore
ear canals. You will not rot, crack, warp
or splinter.

Bus-shat baggage (ecumenical chortle). What drew you to this Trio,
the gurgle or the hiss? Did anyone
warn you?

The vegetables are cheaper, the girls are more willing,
the toilets stink, spring is
everywhere.

                    —after Heine

Marvin Cohen

A Mysterious Case

**SOMETHING INDEFINABLE.
IS IT EVEN FINDABLE?**

"Half in love with easeful Death,"
do I expend my last ounce of breath?
Somehow Death is a great big tease
to put me at a peculiar ease,
almost perverted somehow.
Death and I are on sexual terms,
to fool around with near poison
to drag out a hidden thrill---
from the secret recess of a pill?
(But I don't take any pill.)
Something mysterious is going on,
or is it perhaps some criminal "con"?
All this is far-fetchedly beyond me,
yet close at hand that I can't deduct,
nor with timidity detect.
Certain thoughts are not fully explained,
yet in the barrier between "obscure" and "plain."
My logical mind isn't always there.
It just goes out for a gulp of air.
Then it comes back to the familiar,
but what in the world is THAT?
Don't leave me on the verge of "abstract."
Let's formulate some convivial pact,
and somehow reverse track.
What do I somehow detect?
Is it something in the form of a defect?
What in the world am I getting at?
This is difficult to break down.
Am I a clown? Or just wanting renown?
This is a mysterious case.
How does it start at the base?

**THE ULTIMATE CONTEST,
RESULTED IN A LOP-SIDED CONQUEST.
THIS IS WHAT LIFE POSTHUMOUSLY CONFESSED.**

When Death invades Life's territory,
they combine to become a sad terror story.

Life is terrified and must submit
to Death's cruel takeover bid.
Poor Life! What became of it?
It shrunk and became nothing at all,
for its sports lapse of "dropping the ball."
So Life became immediately disqualified
from the useless luxury of remaining solidified,
having lost retention of its own self
by being fitted into an underground shelf,
having become too old to take good care of itself.
Now buried, the requisite corpse was out of breath,
having raced too hard to elude its fleet chaser, Death.
Flesh shrunk off, and only bones remained
as the permitted bare minimum to be retained.
Result? An overwhelming victory Death gained.
Print that in the "Sporting Chronicle":
a crushing defeat for the Biological.

**NEXT TO THE ROUND CLOCK,
LET YOUR WANDERING BOAT DOCK.
NUMERICALLY TUNE YOURSELF IN
TO WHAT'S CURRENT, IN ORDER TO WIN.**

The clock's only concerns are seconds, minutes, & hours.
Those are its only buds that bear flowers.
It ignores weeks, months, and years,
also centuries and epochs.
So now we know what clocks are for.
Other temporal measurements we can ignore.
Whatever is relevant or pertinent,
concentrate on, one hundred percent.
On consciousness, let those make a dent.
Seconds, minutes, and hours,
concentrate on. They're ours.
Let's also sharply be aware
(other people will want to eagerly share)
of weeks, months, and years.
On those topics, don't be in arrears.
We're all in this boat together.
Let it float in any weather,
depending on where you are,
under the province of this earth's star.
If you're up to date, you'll go far.
All humans, linked in society,
share of the earth's luminous variety.
Along the borders of time and space,
keep your orders, confined in place.

Paolo Pergola

Reference points

WHEN YOU THINK about it, units are simply a system of reference for any kind of measurement. For example, hundreds of years ago, a caveperson must have figured out that one can measure distances based on the length of a foot, and there you have it, you are six feet tall. The same goes for stones, a caveperson must have thought to measure weight using a bunch of regular stones he or she had in some corner of the cave, and there you go, a cave person can weigh ten stones and a mammoth can weigh a hundred stones. In all these cases, you can look at something and say, it's made up of so many feet or stones. Another way to measure something, is to have a standard maximum, like a reference point, which you call one hundred, and whatever you measure is a proportion of that maximum. For example, *oxygen saturation* corresponds to the amount of oxygen traveling through your body with your red blood cells. Ideally, you want to have a hundred percent oxygen-bound hemoglobin in your blood, meaning that your oxygen is being transported in your body. That's good. You need your one-hundred-percent oxygen.

AS FAR AS I am concerned, my reference point, my standard maximum, has always been my uncle. Whatever I did with him, or he did with me, was there for me to compare with anything else I did, when I was a kid, and I still use it to this day. I could give you many examples, one per type of activity, you name it, for example eating, drinking, running, driving, joking, or simply having fun. Let's talk about the subject of having fun, I think this will give you a good idea of what I mean. Summers were fun when I was a kid. It was always hot when I was a kid, but not the kind of hot in which you sweat and you want to change your shirt and you complain and you turn the air conditioning on. Air conditioning did not exist when I was a kid, though it was quite hot. It was that kind of hot when you want to have fun and jump in the waves and invent a sport that you call bodysurfing and it was not about winning or losing, but about riding the waves. And then there was my uncle who, every now and again, would show up at the beach, out of the blue. We knew that he could show up at some point, but for some reason he always came when we least expected it. He had a way to know when that moment had arrived, of being least expected. One day, he showed up directly from the sea, on a motorboat. My brother and I jumped on the boat and we drove away for what must have been a few miles, until we found a little cove on the north side of the Riviera. Only there, did my uncle tell us what the deal was. He pulled out two long wooden bars which we had no idea what they were. Water-skis, that's what they were. That's how we went waterskiing that day with my uncle. We took turns jumping in the water, putting the skis on our feet, and being pulled by the rope attached to the motor boat. Somehow, magically, we rose to the water surface and skimmed along the sea. Sometimes we went in and out of the boat's wake on purpose, and that added even more thrill to the magic. I must have been fourteen or fifteen, I remember thinking—This is *solid fun*, I remember I had so much fun that when I have fun even now, after so many years, I always compare any amount of fun to that waterskiing day with my uncle.

TYPICALLY, any fun activity I do these days is at best forty or fifty percent the fun I had that day, waterskiing. I could watch a movie, a fun movie like a brilliant comedy, then I come out of the movie theater thinking, that was about thirty to forty percent the fun I had that waterskiing day. I could go out for dinner with a bunch of friends, we have pizzas and drink some beer, we chat, we laugh, we stay out until late, and then I am back home, I go to bed, and I think, ok, that was sixty percent the fun I had on that waterskiing day with my uncle, at most. I could go to play tennis with a friend, I may win or lose, it does not matter that much, it's not winning or losing that matters, playing tennis per se can be fun, sure, but not as much fun as that waterskiing day with my uncle. At most, a the fun I have on a nice evening spent playing tennis sums up to about forty percent, of that waterskiing day with my uncle. Anyways, I think you get the idea. That's how I measure fun. My fun-scale.

AND THERE ARE many other fun things my uncle used to do, that's for sure. I could go on forever, if I had to make a list of all the fun things my uncle

used to do, it would be an infinite list that you cannot even measure in feet or in stones. And then there were the pranks. My uncle always came up with the best pranks. He had a way to come up with t h e m when you least expected it. For example, he could fart on command. What he did, he would show me his index finger and would tell me, *Paolo, my finger is jammed, could you pull on it?* I would pull on it, and magically, he would fart. And every time he presented it to me in a different way, so it always worked. And it didn't matter how many times he played that trick on me, every time I fell for it, but it was a fun *falling-for-it* trick. It was the gold standard of all pranks. Impossible to beat, hundred percent pure prank on my prankscale. So, that's how I measure anything that comes along in life, it makes things easier to have a reference point like my uncle. It can be applied to all kinds of things and it's much more precise than the metric system.

Elizabeth Cooperman

Who's Afraid of Contemporary Art?

An Interview with Nora Mapp of Contemporary Art Daily

Elizabeth Cooperman: Contemporary Art Daily is based in Los Angeles, California. How much relationship do you have to the robust art scene in L.A.?

Nora Mapp: Covid has been a strange time. I think we've all adapted to not doing things in person. But the other thing is that because Contemporary Art Daily is committed to showing work from all over the world, we've always tried not to preference the in-person experience, because that would give priority to local shows.

And yet, I have started to go into L.A. to see stuff more. And I find that during the pandemic I've missed texture, and that color feels different when it's physical and not digital. Contemporary Art Daily is about access. I believe you can provide access to ideas without it being physical but seeing work in person also reminds me why I love art, and I think that's a good thing to be reminded of occasionally!

EC: Cheers to that.

NM: Recently I saw a Jeanette Mundt show at Overduin & Co., which is a gallery in L.A., and there was a series of portraits—the same figure reappeared many times, always wearing black stockings. For this series, Mundt had either painted on a rough linen or a rough canvas, but the grain of the canvas with black paint over it recreated almost perfectly what black stockings actually look like. And this was not a style of painting obsessed with the way silk is rippling in the sun or something like that—it wasn't representa-

tional in that way. But it was just a fluke of texture and representation that the grain of the fabric made something that so beautifully mimicked what a stocking is like that it honestly just filled me with joy.

EC: You look at hundreds of images of contemporary art every day for your job. In general, how many given countries are represented in the works of art you see?

NM: Probably thirty to forty.

EC: What parts of the world are represented in that gathering?

NM: We get work from nearly everywhere. That said, we're only seeing art from established galleries or large museums, and that requires an art market and government funding and government support, so the scope is limited to wealthier countries.

EC: What does Contemporary Art Daily do with these images?

NM: About ten years ago, Contemporary Art Daily started featuring two international exhibitions a day, and the site has been going strong ever since.

Recently, we created an offshoot of CAD called Contemporary Art Library. For the library we're accepting much more work. It's more of an archival project than a curatorial project.

EC: You work from home, as lots of people have been doing during the pandemic. What do you see from your home office?

NM: My house looks out onto live oak trees that almost resemble olive trees, so kind of dusty green trees. The leaves are tough here because of being desert plants.

EC: Tell me more about Topanga Canyon, which you call home. It's outside of Los Angeles, and a pretty wild place!

NM: People assume that a lot of us who work in "culture" live in a city, and then inevitably that we live in apartments that kind of resemble galleries—white apartments with white walls. But I live in a place that, for one, is not the city. Topanga Canyon is architecturally and weather-wise so *warm*—totally unlike the neutral aesthetic of a gallery, or the aesthetic of Contemporary Art Daily's website, which is minimal and clean and rigorously curated and very related to the white cube.

It sounds almost ridiculous to say, but I live in a wooden cabin with an outdoor kitchen, and an outdoor bathtub under an apple tree. The cabin was part of a commune built in the '80s by this strange person who left the world of advertising to start building houses. He was reclaiming wood from the Santa Monica Pier before it was trendy to reclaim wood, and he was getting hardware from the L.A. utility dump. What I love about this place is that there are trees everywhere here, and nothing is straight—no line or piece of wood is straight.

Also, my dog died a couple of months ago, and I love getting to spend time with my neighbor's dog every day. It comes over and says hi and barks at my deck and wants to come up to my house.

EC: Famously, Neil Young lived in Topanga Canyon, and the band Canned Heat, and lots of other artists and weirdos . . .

NM: I don't know anything about Canned Heat, but Topanga's always been this kind of surfer-shack enclave. There's weird architecture all over this canyon. Unlike the mentality of downtown L.A., the aesthetic in Topanga seems to be about using whatever materials are nearby and cheap.

There's an architect I've loved for years called Fu Sujimoto, and I think about him a lot. He built a wooden cabin, and he decided on a thickness of board. The logs aren't round like a log cabin, they're rectilinear. So it's kind of like—what's that game where you're pulling pieces of wood out?

EC: Jenga?

NM: Jenga! Yeah, Fujimoto's cabin is kind of like a Jenga cabin. It's like a cube made from these Jenga pieces, and all divisions inside the cabin—the stairs, bed platform, table—they're just made from levels of wood that an inhabitant can use various ways. What's the table can also be the bed, what's the stairs can also be a shelf. At the time Fujimoto was building this cabin, he related architecture to living in caves. So, it's like you're surrounded by surfaces, and you can decide what those surfaces are good for, what they're comfortable for, and they can be anything. And in a way, I think that's very much how I live. When I come back from swimming in the morning, I have a bowl of hot soup, and I use the bottom stair of my deck as a table because that's where the sun hits at that hour. I'm on my computer all day, but I'm also very aware of *being* in the day, because I'm really exposed to the elements in this ridiculous glass and wood cabin and wood deck here, and I'm constantly shifting my position around the property based on the warmth and brightness and glare of the sun. It's a funny life. It's both very online and very much outdoors and physical.

EC: Are contemporary artists working in any mediums that would surprise us? What current trends are you seeing right now at Contemporary Art Daily and Library?

NM: Hmm . . . a lot of artists are working with furniture actually. And I've also noticed an outpouring of textile work right now—so tapestries, or cloth, or yarn, or using fabric. For a long time, textiles were really gendered, but that has changed. Textiles have reached a level of recognition where men are using them, too. They've really taken on a painterly role. There's some amazing work happening.

EC: Is there an example that comes to mind?

NM: I'm thinking of Anthony Olubunmi Akinbola, this young male artist who uses bright pink in his work. I almost see it as painting, even though he uses fabric, both folded and woven. The fabric serves as a kind of monochrome painting, but it's all about texture. And so, brush stroke is being replaced by fabric drape.

It's not sculpture—but, like sculptors, textile artists get to utilize the power of materials to add information and context: like, this is a blanket from my grandmother, who had such-and-such history, and such-and-such background, and such-and-such geography, and she was from this region, and this yarn is from this region, and so every material choice has a history and carries information.

And at the same time, these textile works have the advantage of being two-dimensional, hanging on the wall, so they're being read in the realm of painting, and the history of painting. But they also have this added historical/material context.

EC: As a person who aspires to someday own a herd of alpaca, I love the sound of this. Making "paintings" from their wool. Can you describe another example for me?

NM: Rodney McMillian uses crocheted blankets and kind of deteriorates them or adds onto them. When I say crochet, these pieces read very obviously as something thrown over a sofa which has then been put on the wall and can be read in quite a few different ways. Both artists I'm thinking of are men. Again, textile work has been subcategorized forever as a lesser form than painting, and less of an art form than a craft—I'm partly thinking of *my* mother here, who is a quilter.

EC: So, does McMillian literally take a blanket his grandmother made and put it on the wall, like you would a found object, or is he working the materials?

NM: All these contemporary textile artists are working the materials, I believe. It's just that their materials have a kind of intimacy.

One of the most significant qualities of paint is its utter neutrality. It is really nothing. And that's why so many painters are obsessed with the idea of the "frame," and the shape of the canvas, and the texture, and then the brush stroke, etc.

Traditional forms of artmaking use a neutral material to make something that is *not* neutral, as opposed to today where it's much more common to take a highly charged object (or material) to make an even more highly charged object.

EC: Can you say more about that?

NM: Hair is a good example. There's a longtime practice of words or images shaved into people's heads, and the James Bantone show last year in Zurich was a play on that. The skull can be a template, either for tattoos or for ubiquitous but incredibly talented barber shop forms of expression—in Black culture especially—and so Bantone's show was kind of a play on what can be done in thinking about long hair as a blank page.

In several photos from that show, you see long hair with an ombre effect in the background, like red to black, or red to green. So, you have hair as simply a kind of colorful background—a background for words—but it's a background that is *loaded*, with meaning. Instead of just neutral paint with an ombre effect, you see that this is a person, this is a person with hair, this is a person who's probably Black, this is a person who has culture, whose hair has culture, whose hair has meaning, and then words are added on top of all that meaning, and those words are applied with neon puffy paint, which is also nontraditional!

EC: There's a dog barking at you.

NM: I know, I'm hanging out with my neighbor Tulip, and she sees our other neighbor Silver up on the hill, and she's worked up about this.

EC: Topanga neighbors for ya . . .

NM: It's an animal safari here!

EC: Ha! Your job focuses on contemporary art, but is there a period of art that you personally go back to and love?

NM: I'm really a generalist, and I've come to love contemporary art, but many years ago I was interested in the Protestant Reformation.

EC: Say more . . .

NM: I was interested in how Protestant churches were being whitewashed and how, at the same time, there was a change in the economy of Europe that occurred because of a rising merchant class that was also Protestant, and who did not want religious images (because those images were incorrect, according to their beliefs). They were the ones going to these newly whitewashed churches.

EC: They didn't want iconography.

NM: They didn't want any iconography, and for the first time in the Western world since the Greeks, there's an opening for paintings that are not about religion. Suddenly people want portraits of their wives, and people want portraits of themselves, and people want art to say things like, I'm wealthy, or I have a beautiful wife because I'm wealthy.

EC: Look at my belly! . . .

NM: Exactly! They want art to say, I can eat so much foie gras, I'm so happy and wealthy, invest in my shipping business.

And similarly, they were like, I'll buy a painting of apples on the table, or I'll buy a painting of a bouquet of flowers because that would look good in my house.

EC: So, this is Rembrandt's time?

NM: This is Rembrandt, yeah, this is heading from the Renaissance into Mannerism, into the fifteenth and sixteenth centuries, and there was just this opening where painters could depict different things for the first time in Judeo-Christian Western Europe.

But prior to the Reformation, one feature of Christian art is that it had created a set of symbols that were used over and over and over again—a lily meant Christ, a lamb meant Christ . . .

EC: Blue meant Mary . . .

NM: Exactly. And because of that, everyday people had a lot of tools for looking at these paintings in church. And many of these people were not literate, but they knew these stories and the paintings had an agreed upon formal language.

Once the Protestant Reformation started breaking up the need to remake the same religious stories over and over, artists had to create new tools of communication. With each painting, you had to create a *new* way for a viewer to understand what you were trying to communicate. And I think in many ways we are still in that place . . .

EC: Hmm.

NM: It's a really interesting place to be, but it's very, very, very difficult for both the artist and the viewer, to have this burden of remaking how to talk to each other with every new work that we see.

EC: So, you're saying that we're still in the Reformation?

NM: In a way, yes, I think so. We're still in a place where there's no agreed upon language because there's no agreed upon style—like Ab-Ex is not the rule of the day. Nothing is the rule of the day. There's never been fewer rules, there's never been more inclusivity, which is great, but it means that . . .

EC: You start over every time.

NM: Yeah, the onus to communicate has to be "made new" every single time. And this lack of baseline communication is difficult, and I think it's one of things that turns people off to contemporary art.

EC: Do people like contemporary art?

NM: No. People don't like contemporary art, they don't know how to read it, they're afraid of it, they're insecure near it, they don't know what to think, they don't have the tools for it. And I think a lot of that is because there's no set of tools anymore. And that's very hard, and it makes it really niche.

But when people tell me they're turned off by contemporary art, I just say, your opinion matters. You can like something or not like something. Or you can read what an artist has to say about their work at the gallery or museum and then look at the work, and be interested or not interested in the work, and that's valid. You don't have to feel invalidated by what you're looking at.

EC: Speaking of, I noticed that you've featured the work of the artist Lily van der Stokker on your site many times over the years, and I have trouble knowing what I'm supposed to feel when I look at her work. Do you admire her?

NM: I do, and one of the things I've enjoyed about her work is that I kind of misread her when I was younger. When I started to understand her more, I just remember feeling a joy that gestures I'd taken to be ironic were actually incredibly earnest. I'm thinking of a phrase that was the title of one of her shows a couple years ago, which was "friendly good."

EC: What good?

NM: *Friendly* good. Her color palette is very bright; it's very nine-year-old girl, like in the best sort of way. She uses this huge bubble text. Everything is cute; everything is sort of like lushly pleasant. She's asserting that there's intellectual room for friendly goodness in the world. That it deserves museum space. I realized that really distinguished her work from most of the feminist work done in the 90s. She wasn't taking an aggressive stance. She was insisting that this "friendly goodness" wasn't just about cuteness or prettiness or bubbly flowers—that friendliness de-

served not just aesthetic room but that it had value, both formally and conceptually.

EC: But what really is "friendly goodness"?

NM: To me, friendly goodness is a flower on a wall, a flower that's rendered, and friendly goodness is always in this soft bubble font—it's images, it's words, it's recipes written out, it's what we might associate with plastic furniture from the children's area of Ikea with soft legs that are all a little plump, kind of like elephant legs, and orange tables. It's a funny aesthetic. It's an aesthetic that's easy to demean as belonging in a child's bedroom.

EC: Almost a bit horrifying, isn't it? Friendliness—ahh!

NM: It can be! But I realized that it's easy to demean that space as either childlike or feminine, and when I understood her work better I found it incredibly exciting and powerful that she was taking this stance that ideas don't have to be aggressive, and that ideas don't have to be intellectually difficult, nor do formal shapes have to be aggressive or intellectually difficult, that this is part of our world, and it's beautiful, and it makes you feel good, and it's soft, and I'm gonna celebrate it.

EC: And it's not shocking . . .

NM: Actually, I think that idea *is* shocking in the context of the art world—to say this deserves space on the wall, quite literally. But, it's not shocking to our eyes. Like many readymades, van der Stokker took something that was kind of normalized in a completely different context—I'm going to bring up the cliché of Duchamp—and she brought it into the museum, and it *is* shocking to give value to this aesthetic which had always been demeaned.

EC: It's interesting that the gesture of the ready-made keeps happening in different ways in the art world long after Duchamp's urinal.

NM: Well, in the end a museum or a gallery is architecture that serves as a frame—as a cultural frame—and when you frame things (whether it's a really annoying Italian cinematographer who's taking his own fingers and pointing at things in his film, or whether it's a urinal or a bubbly flower), that white space, that cultural authority, acts as a framing system for people to look at things in a different way. And artists have used that for readymades, but artists have used that for everything. To ask: how do we think of things now?

EC: When you're sifting through images for Contemporary Art Daily, do you ever get the sense that there are people out there who strive to be among the avant-garde? In a Duchampian sense, I guess.

NM: I don't find myself thinking about the avant-garde very much, at Contemporary Art Daily or in general. In a very realistic way, artists are trying so hard to survive. In a way, being avant-garde has always been a terrible career choice! And yeah, the truth is that people are trying to do the work they care about while not being so ahead of their time that they don't fit anywhere.

Artists who have big gallery and museum shows are part of an establishment, and so the avant-garde culture is probably something that I don't see that much in my job. The avant-garde are likely the friends of the people who are slightly more mainstream—and that's always how it's been.

EC: Not to sound too lofty, but, ahem, let me clear my throat . . . I've been thinking about the trajectory of art history in Western civilization, and I was planning to ask you whether we are post-abstraction yet.

NM: No.

EC: Or how many steps away from post-abstraction might we be in painting, let's say?

NM: We're still in a place where everything is possible. Everything is on the table. But abstraction is happening in different ways, for instance the textile work we talked about—

thinking about abstraction through texture as opposed to just shape and just brush stroke. I won't say anything about post-abstraction. I don't think that will happen any time soon. Abstraction is still very much something contemporary artists think about.

EC: I guess abstraction is useful to us as human beings.

NM: Exactly, and then going back and forth is very useful.

Actually, there's a huge flowering of realism in the painting world right now. Like gothic imagery. All this gorgeous, somber, gothic almost grotesquerie. Really beautiful medieval vibes are coming out. Very moody. But very figural, very realistic. Lots of painters are really thinking about *not* abstraction. And that's been so exciting to see! That wasn't happening back when I was in art school.

EC: I love the idea of this gothic revival.

NM: Totally. Anyone who has spent a lot of time looking at art in old European churches would really like some of these new medieval-y-toned paintings. I went to a show this week at House of Gaga by a young Mexican painter named Karla Kaplun. She made a series of fifteen to twenty paintings in wood frames, all close together, all touching, as if remaking the wall of a large church. It's basically a large altarpiece. And she relates directly to religious iconography. She's using what are the classical painting techniques—she's using "the shine," she's painting on wood, she's using sheer layers of oil paint, she's using varnish after oil paint—and it's luminous and stylistically *very* similar to Renaissance styles and artistic techniques but the stories are all different.

EC: Fantastic . . . Okay, bear with me, because I want to change gears again.

NM: Okay, ha! I'm not sure if this interview has a through-line . . .

EC: That's okay. It may not! But I want to talk about art and death now, which is the ultimate through-line, isn't it?

NM: I guess so!

EC: Okay, I've been thinking a lot about the disposability of art. After we die, what happens to all the art we made? I mean like physically. In an interview, the artist R.H. Quaytman talked about how her stepfather was a sculptor who left all these enormous works behind in a storage unit when he died, and Quaytman underlined that one of the problems of being an artist, from a practical standpoint, is the physical trace you leave behind.

What happens to the hardbound journals I keep so passionately once they're not useful to anyone anymore? What happens to enormous museum installation pieces that took years to construct once the culture no longer values those installations, once they no longer surprise or shock us? At what point do museum's run out of storage and start weeding through the art, throwing it in the landfill? Decades from now, how much of today's art will pass someone's Marie Kondo does-it-spark-joy test?

So, my very circuitous question for you is, at Contemporary Art Daily, where you face a daily onslaught of art, sort of like this river flowing into your inbox every day, do you ever feel depressed about the disposability of art, as I'm inclined to feel? Or maybe it's the opposite for you? Maybe you feel a daily surge of energy?

NM: I think I feel both on different days . . . It can often be too much, and exhausting—like oh my God, another fucking installation—of which there are a lot less these days, by the way. It's really great! No one wants to look at installation art anymore, thank God.

But back to your original question, that river of creative work sometimes feels heavy and difficult and sometimes feels really inspiring.

EC: That makes sense.

NM: There's a great beauty in that river that you spoke of, just this onslaught and this flow of people and images and ideas, but like any amount of beauty, you kind of have to turn off after a while. Like, I drove back from Big Sur yesterday, and it's a drive that's so phenomenally beautiful that you could stop at every single curve of the road, but eventually you just have to keep driving.

EC: Totally.

NM: On the plus side, I'm part of something beautiful, which is: people are thinking and making and choosing to live their lives creating art.

EC: Which brings me to my last question. Why contemporary art?

NM: What do you mean?

EC: Just, why should we pay attention to it? Think of all the incredible Renaissance art you alluded to, for example, which is sitting around in old churches waiting for us.

NM: Why? Because contemporary art is what's alive. It's not what's easy. Things that have already been curated, already been authorized—that's easier. That's much tidier. We already know what's good and not good.

But contemporary *is* because this is life *now*. And it's not easy. And you look at a lot of bad stuff with good stuff, and you don't even know what's good or bad, and you don't even know what matters—because it's *all* alive. And that is in fact what matters. Not what's good or bad.

EC: Right, we're in the middle of it and we can't see it and there's so much opportunity to choose how we want to see.

NM: Yes, there's a different process at work when you look at a verified master like Rafael, let's say. There's something much messier and muddier and more complex about dealing with what our contemporaries are thinking about.

When we were talking about recent trends in contemporary art, I was remembering that a couple of years ago people were really into bird cages.

EC: Huh?

NM: And I do enjoy watching these larger trends play out, which might get back to the vanguard or avant-garde. You often can't tell that much about what's in the zeitgeist by the forerunner or the genius, but you can really tell by how many, many, many people take those ideas and rework them, and then you see that something about someone's birdcage has become really important to a lot of people—to the point where it's like, wow, artists are really thinking about that material. Why *is* that?

EC: Right, the birdcage is resonating.

NM: And again, it's interesting to me that the derivative stuff can in a way be more articulate about what's happening and what people care about, sometimes more than the forerunners.

EC: Because you might not recognize the forerunners.

NM: Exactly. *I'm* a contemporary. So, I don't know what's happening . . .

EC: . . . In the future.

NM: Right! And I think that's a great argument for the contemporary—that you are not seeing it through a historical lens. You haven't been fed a story. Often, we don't know until later, or we don't know until someone like [Clement] Greenberg puts the label on it, and then art history students ever after have a name for the era. People in Rafael's time weren't necessarily looking at his work as this hallowed thing.

EC: True.

NM: It was like, another thing in a church.

EC: So, it seems like the beauty of contemporary art for you is that it's yet to be defined.

NM: After studying a lot of art history and seeing only the best of the best, yes, it's been exciting to see how much value there is in things that *aren't* the best—in art that's average.

EC: Sometimes it just blows my mind that people don't stop . . . they don't stop making art! They don't stop coming up with new ways to paint a sunflower, or a sunset, or a birdcage. They'll paint a poem on a head of hair. It's mind-blowing, in a way, and it's also almost boring after a while . . .

NM: Right, there's something in humans that can't say, "painting is dead." We just can't. It can't be dead. It's clearly not. And many, many decades have proved that. Artists have proved what a valid, fruitful, endlessly open format painting is, and that we need that. And that whatever blankness exists, there's a desire to fill it.

All that said, I've never understood graffiti, even though I know it comes from the same impulse. And it's so appalling to see people carve into trees, which is somehow similar to this desire to make marks.

Recently I was taking my daily hike in Topanga, and at the top of the mountain, someone had taken out pieces of moss on a stone in the shape of a smiley face—so the moss grew over into this smiley face. And then a few days later, I saw it on another rock, and I was like, fuck this! I don't want to see an image on this rock. And so, I literally found the pieces of moss on the ground that someone had removed, and I replaced them, so that the moss would grow back smooth, and I felt really happy about the image-making on my part!

EC: Brilliant.

Ryan Ruby

Context Collapse 4

HSIN JIH JIH HSIN: Modernism's motto
May have first appeared as an inscription
On the bathtub of Emperor Ch'eng T'ang
A thousand years before the alphabet
Arrives in Greece, but, as ideas are wont
To do, it reemerges in the early
20th century[1] to serve needs closer
At hand, viz., *product differentiation*[2]
On a glutted literary market
More and more subject to the centrifugal

[1] In his engaging book on the concept
of novelty in philosophy, science,
and art, Michael North meticulously
reconstructs the history of "Make It New,"
noting that, despite quasi-mythicizing
accounts by scholars like Kenner, Frye, and Rahv,
the phrase does not appear in Pound's work until
1928, well after the first wave
of high modernism had receded.
Still, there is enough contemporaneous
evidence to demonstrate, however
one dates these three words in particular,
that the spirit that animated them
was entirely representative.
    Virginia Woolf, it will be remembered,
famously dates a sea-change in "human
character" to "on or about December
1910." Three years later, in *Perchè
sono Futurista*, Giovanni
Papini lists the search for novelty
as one of the characteristic features
of the movement. A March 1916
entry from Hugo Ball's diary reads:
*Seien wir neu und erfinderisch von Grund
aus. Dichten wir das Leben täglich um.*
And this, from 1918, is the torso
of Apollo: *Du mußt dein Leben ändern!*
    For other cognate usages, please see
Jed Rasula's article "Make it New,"
published in *Modernism/modernity*.

[2] Whether this should be considered *vertical*
or *horizontal* differentiation
is one of the intractable problems
of aesthetics. It will not be resolved
here. (Or anywhere else, for that matter.)

Pressures of mechanical reproduction
And a pronounced intensification
Of the intergenerational struggle
Between *tradition and the individual
Talent*,[3] occasioned (in part) by improved
Methods for storing and distributing

[3] Since words like *original* and *authentic*
are no longer applied with a straight face
to works of art, it is worth reminding
ourselves why they mattered so much to poets
between, roughly, the eras of Milton
and Stevens. Whether consciously or not,
these poets conceived of themselves as soldiers
fighting on two fronts (against the past, against
the future; or in techno-economic
terms, against *redundancy* and *obsolescence*
respectively). The Oedipal logic
of immortality, which continues
long after the death of romanticism,
forbids belatedness and impresses
upon poets a "horror of finding
[themselves] to be a copy or replica"
relative to their precursors, that is,
finding themselves to be redundant persons
whose poems are buried with their bodies
(if not, as often happens, well before then)
both of which *might as well have never been.*
    The same logic forbids supersession
by poets as yet unborn, whose achievements
threaten a fantastic reversal of time,
making it seem as though the later poet
has written the earlier poet's lines.
(See Bloom, *The Anxiety of Influence.*
Citing Bloom in this context is almost
obligatory, though he considers
belatedness solely w/r/t
developments internal to poetry,
rather than as a matter of the broader
culture of the copy that comes to surround
and suffocate it, the approach pursued here,
though the very notion of "developments
internal to poetry" is *prima
facie* evidence for the increasing
autonomy of the poetic field,
which is not, it should go without saying,
primarily internal to poetry.)
    Among the more popular tactics that were
employed to wage this war is the notion
that originality could be secured
if a poet's language was *of its time*—
which is clearly visible in the passage
by Eliot quoted below—but as
it is technology and not language

Texts,[4] and (in part) by the establishment
Of departments for the regulation
And study of national literatures
At universities across Europe
And North America over the course
Of the preceding fifty-or-so years.

Having already secured copyright,
Poets are incentivized to develop
A trademark 'voice' or *style*,[5] which, in turn,
Contributes to a proliferation
Of innovative formal devices[6]
Also aimed at *defamiliarizing*
Language for a dwindling consumer base
Whose experience of modern life[7] had taught
It how to assimilate the shocking

which sets the pace of temporality
in high and late capitalist cultures
this emphasis on the present will turn out
to be shortsighted, condemning writers
to serve the same communications platforms
they would use to disseminate their writing,
as will be shown a little further on.

[4] Result: the supply curve shifts to the right.

[5] Depending on whether the preferred self-
conception is that of inspired bard
or impersonal craftsman, a division
that will track, though somewhat inexactly,
the schism between what Charles Bernstein calls
official verse culture and the avant-garde,
and which, when professionalization
completely colonizes American
poetry, will inform the pedagogy
of and hiring practices at various
competing creative writing departments.

[6] Incl, but hardly limited to:
collage, intertextual allusion,
automatic writing, repetitiveness,
temporal displacement, stream-of-consciousness,
"mythic method," and of course the kinds of
idiosyncratic lineation,
orthography and punctuation licensed
by the prestige now accorded to Whitman.

[7] With its mechanized wars, its revolutions
both political and scientific
and its apparently endless Fordist stream
of new products. Of these, the automobile
and the airplane are the most consequential,
but special mention deserves to be made

To the habitual at a stunning pace,
Numbing it to all but the most novel
Stimuli.[8] Although this had the general
Effect of rendering poetic language
[T]rudnyy, zatrudnennyy, zatormozhennyy,[9]
Modernist inaccessibility
Should not be conflated with the anti-art
Provocations of contemporaneous
Avant-gardes (e.g., Futurism, Dada).[10]

of the new technical media, starting
with Friedrich Kittler's fin de siècle
trinity: Gramophone—Film—Typewriter.

[8] Film would come to exert the same downward
pressure on the novel on that the novel
 once exerted on narrative poetry,
externalizing its proprietary
'hallucination'-function. Faced with this threat,
the novel makes a tactical retreat
into the form's unfilmable features,
interiority and abstraction.
When obsolescence becomes medium-
specific, the novel becomes poetic,
and poetry, pushed further to the margins
of culture, crosses the margin of language
itself, into *terra incognita*.

[9] In the words of critic Viktor Shklovsky.
Eliot states the case in similar terms:

> We can . . . say that it appears . . . that poets
> in our civilization, as it
> exists at present, must be difficult.
> Our civilization comprehends
> great variety and complexity
> and this variety and complexity . . .
> must produce various and complex results.
> [Accordingly] the poet must become
> more and more comprehensive, more allusive,
> more indirect, in order to force, to
> dislocate if necessary, language
> into his meaning. [Twit twit twit / Jug jug
> jug jug jug jug / So rudely forc'd. / Tereu]

[10] To name only a pair of the dozens
of ismistic movements which were founded
and just as suddenly vanished during
the First World War and the years that followed.
    The growth of so-called literary 'schools'
can be traced to the High Middle Ages,
as a means of distributing the risks
associated with being a sole
proprietor in an expanding market,
that is, among those, who, for any number
of possible reasons, did not receive
the backing of royal academies,

While it is true that what distinguishes
Pound and Possum in London from Tzara
And Hugo 'Der Magischer Bischof' Ball
At the Cabaret Voltaire in Zurich,
Velimir 'Korol Vremeni' Khlebnikov
At the Stray Dog Café in Petersburg,
Or Marinetti in his totaled Fiat,
Has less to do, all told, with their respective
Programs than with the means according to which
These were to be realized, this fact should not
Be minimized either. As their analogues
In politics were soon to discover
Kleine Differenzen entscheiden über
Leben und Tod. Anglophone modernism,
Esp. in its classical mode,
Ramifies the poem, complicates it,
Occulting its meanings, which are at once
Overdetermined and indeterminate,
But to the precise extent that a poem
Calls for exegesis to be understood,
Its attempts at communication are
Genuine. Even when the signals sent
Can only be received-as-intended
By a self-selecting semi-public—
A caste of fellow poets, connoisseurs,[11]

risks that would become—thanks to developments
in the international financial
system starting roughly in the transition
between Baudelaire's Deuxième Empire
and the Troisième République of Rimbaud,
and continuing, despite at least two
significant interruptions, until
the present—extremely acute. Bourdieu:
> . . . il ne suffit pas à determiner
> le rassemblement en corps, condition
> de l'apparition de l'effet de corps
> dont les groupes littéraires et artistiques
> les plus fameux ont tiré d'immenses profites
> symboliques, jusque par et dans les ruptures
> plus ou moins éclatantes qui y ont mis fin.

[11] Literary modernism revived
some of the features associated
with pre-modern cultural economies,
but as Lawrence Rainey shows, patronage,
as it then existed, constituted
a circuit within the capitalist marketplace
rather than a system in its own right.

Professional critics, and professors[12]—
Its portfolio is still diversified,
As it retains investments in rhetoric.

The Futurists and Dadaists, by contrast,
Seeking a wider audience (humankind)[13]

     Patrons (or more often, patronesses)
couched their activities in the current
language of investment and collection,
that is, in the language of the art world,
whose "artisanal mode of production
is compatible with a limited
submarket for luxury goods." The need
to "concretize the literary, to turn
it into an object . . . that could genuinely
rise in value" explains the prominence
of deluxe or limited editions
in the early publishing histories
of the touchstones of modernist writing—
and perhaps even the theories behind
Imagism and Objectivism.
Already precarious, the patron-
investor circuit was terminally
disrupted by the 1929
Wall Street Crash, which sent Eliot fleeing
into the bosom of the Church, and Pound
into the outstretched arm of *Il Duce*.

[12] If one were inclined to be cynical,
one might allude to the symbiotic
relationship that could be said to exist
between *difficulty* and *hermeneutics*:
a poem whose meaning is not clear invites
explication and explication in turn
ensures the longevity of the poem.
What the difficult poet sacrifices
in the spatial distribution of her
readership—which shrinks in number—she gains
in the temporal extension of her work.
     But is there really any evidence
that this was a conscious strategem? *Yes*:
     If I gave it all up immediately,
     I'd lose my immortality. I've put
     in so many enigmas and puzzles
     that it *will keep the professors busy*
     for centuries arguing over what I
     meant, and that's the only way of insuring
     one's immortality. (emphasis added)
     Hannah Sullivan is right to point out
that what made Anglophone modernism
one of—if not the—most successful movements
in the history of literature
is that "*it was just difficult enough*."

[13] Not that, in doing so, they pandered to it
in any way. Far from it! Where the public

For their 'primitivist' rites of renewal,[14]
Force language in the opposite direction:
Following in the footsteps of Cratylus,
Who once failed to convince the wisest man
In Athens that the relationship between
The signifier and the signified
Is inherently *mimological*,
They begin by reifying lexis,
Then speed through *telegraphic compression*[15]

is concerned, their respective positions
might be summed up by the subtle chasm
between the slogan of the *Little Review*
edited by Margaret Anderson
and the name of the Russo-Futurist
Hylaea Group's founding manifesto.

[14] Among antebellum intellectuals,
pacifists and militarists alike,
the sense that rationality was leading
to Europe's decline was widespread. In dance,
painting, sculpture, theater, as well as
poetry, vampiric regeneration
was sought in the 'Adamic' cultural
practices and objects of its peasantry
or its overseas colonies, Africa
in particular. The result—taking
Dadaist works like *Gadji beri bimba*
and *chants nègres* as paradigms—were acts
of appropriation and minstrelsy
that make today's iterations seem almost
ethically-sourced by comparison.
     And while futurist-primitivism
is obviously an oxymoron,
this hardly prevented its devotees
from espousing it. That they were disinclined
to look to Africa for precedents
says more about their views about precedents
than about their views about Africans,
which were perhaps even more regressive
than those of their colleagues in Switzerland.
To paraphrase Umberto Boccioni:
     L'Europa può essere molto
     primitiva—aspetta e vedrai!

[15] The specific formulation is Goll's,
but, as John J. White, in his monograph
Literary Futurism, demonstrates,
the metaphor was very much "in the air"
at the time. Nearly all of the poets
considered here relied on it at one point
or another to describe their technique—
as did Apollinaire, Cendrars, Auden,
Wyndham Lewis and Franz Richard Behrens.
     Interestingly enough, *Telegrammstil*,
as the latter called it, was sometimes seen

En route to unintelligibility,
From whence the distance to an *aesthetics*
Of silence[16] is almost negligible.
    Just as a molecule might undergo
Exothermic reaction, the sign, too,
Is decomposed—optophonetically[17]—
Into its *material* components,
The phoneme and the grapheme,[18] which are then
Polarized, generating, on the one hand,
Lautgedichte,[19] and on the other, *Marked Texts*,
The aptly named Johanna Drucker's name
For the graphic design innovations
Facilitated by Mergenthaler's

as an economizing, time-saving
device for the harried modern reader.
Once again, the effect of media
technology on form is apparent:
from the beginning, writing had abolished
proximity as a prerequisite
for communication—at the expense
of a (sometimes significant) delay;
now, with the telegraph and telephone,
communication could occur anywhere
in the world—and instantaneously, too.

[16] Vis-à-vis the size of the audience,
this would amount to an almost perfect
dialectical reversal into
nothingness. "Ambivalence about
making contact with the audience" is how
Susan Sontag explains the situation,
which is, furthermore, "a leading motif
in modern art, with its tireless commitment
to the 'new'." Cf. Fn. 64.

[17] To use Raoul Hausmann's terminology.

[18] In *Sein und Zeit*, Heidegger reminds us
that, as most of our knowledge of equipment
is pre-theoretical, it is only
when our tools break that we actually
start to notice their constituent parts.
Later, in his Parmenides lectures,
he will go on to say, that, where language
is concerned, perhaps no single factor
is more responsible for its breakdown
than the invention of the typewriter.
In any case, a materialist
ontology of the sign is the premise
on which almost every bad inference
made by the avant-garde has since been based.

[19] A generic category broad enough
to encompass such acoustic artifacts
as Futurist mechanomatopoeia,

Linotype machine.[20] Alas, both movements
Lacked the courage of their semiotic
Convictions. No sooner had they attempted
To strangle every semantic convention
They could lay their fingers on, than they were gripped
By the need to explain why they had done so,
In bombastic sentences that nonetheless
Satisfied all the requirements of sense.
As a consequence, the genre for which
They are remembered is the *manifesto*,
For those prose *supplements* their poems leaned
On as a shell-shocked soldier leans on his crutch;

the transrational glossolalia
of Aleksei Kruchenykh and Khlebnikov,
Edith Sitwell's Jabberwockish abstractions,
Dadaist simultaneous poems
and faux-Africanisms (see above)
and Baroness von Freytag-Loringhoven's
plangent deathwail. While such investigations
yielded rather homogeneous outcomes,
taken together, they had the virtue
of restoring verse to its autochthonous
context as kind of oral performance.
    Why, however, they ought to be defined
as poetry—in anything other
than an institutional sense—is quite
unclear. There is, let's not forget, a term
for 'verse without words': *Music*. At least Schwitters
acknowledges this with the title of his
celebrated contribution to the form.
See Rasula, *Destruction* and White, *op. cit.*
    That being said, if you were to argue
that *there is no such thing as poetry*
except in an institutional sense,
and thus the question has been begged against
sound poetry, you wouldn't be wrong either.

[20] With dynamic layouts and variable
font sizes and typefaces—combined here
and there with handwritten script—the Dadaists
and Futurists, both Italian and Russian,
along with the Soviet Constructivists
challenged the spatial assumptions of print,
calling further attention to the page
as physical object and, by extension,
reading as a material process.
    Their influence, however, was most strongly
felt, not in poetry, but in commercial
graphic design, where it revolutionized
the look of advertisements and posters.
For a fuller treatment of the print-based
art practices of the teens and twenties,
and their relation to the ad industry,
see Drucker's study *The Visible Word*.

For paratexts, in a word, more than for texts,[21]
As might have been (and indeed was) foreseen.[22]
If one were searching for a synthesis
Between these tendencies, one could be found
In the writings of Gertrude Stein, who ought
—More than Joyce, Proust, Kafka, or even Pound—
To be regarded as the century's
Preeminent literary figure.

[21] As Apollinaire pithily remarked:
. . . les futuristes viennent nous apprendre—
par leurs titres et non par leurs oeuvres . . .
Defined by Genette as the material
surrounding the published text—incl.
the title, cover, front matter, preface,
and footnotes as well as promotional
materials like blurbs and interviews—
the paratext provides the immediate
context for a work of literature,
the threshold of [its] *interpretation,*
and cannot be excluded from any
full consideration of its reception
and therefore its meaning, much to the chagrin
of New Critical theory and practice.

[22] Like any edifice built on unsound
theoretical foundations, this one's
collapse was all-but-inevitable.
     Communication, being a social
phenomenon, is made possible by
mutually agreed-upon rules. Destroy
these and you destroy what they enable,
involving you, should you wish to persist,
in a performative contradiction.
     ". . . in [the modern artist's] renunciation
of 'society' one cannot fail to
perceive a highly social gesture," notes
Sontag. Marinetti conceded the point
in *Distruzione della sintassi*:
     La filosofia, le scienze . . .
     la politica, il giornalismo,
     l'insegnamento, gli affari, pur
     ricercando forme sintetiche di
     espressione, dovranno ancora
     valersi della sintassi . . . Sono
     costretto infatti, a servirmi
     di tutto ciò per potervi
     esporre la mia concezione.
Truth be told, *parole in libertà*
did not go as far as they might have done
—as the Dadaists did, for example,
or as MacLeish did in *Ars Poetica*,
when he wrote, "A poem should not mean / But be"—
to accomplish Marinetti's stated goal.
  His poems, like their telegraphic models,

You disagree?[23] Well, then. Consider that
1. The laboratory observations
Of her first published work, a medical
Paper ("Normal Motor Automatism")
Co-authored with Leon M. Solomons,
Under the supervision of William
James and the German psychotechnician
Hugo Münsterberg, while she was a student
At Radcliffe College,[24] precedes similar
Investigations into the nature
Of consciousness and its implications
For literature by Simone Rachel Kahn,
Georgie Hyde-Lees, and both of their husbands

are parasitic on an understanding
of ordinary (Italian) spelling
and grammar for their expressive effects.
White calls it an "alternative syntax,"
which cuts the slogan down to its proper size.

[23] If so, don't worry: her contemporaries
didn't know what to make of her either.
    The leading critic of the day was prescient
enough to devote a chapter to her work
in his landmark study of 'symbolist
writing'—Pound didn't make the cut—but in it
he confesses to having been unable
to finish her masterpiece and concludes
—begrudgingly or far too charitably
depending on your point of view—
that even if Stein was "widely ridiculed . . .
seldom enjoyed" and thus "read less and less"
(a judgment that, with the publication
of the *Autobiography* two years
later, would prove almost comically false)
she was nonetheless a "literary
personality of unmistakable
originality and distinction,"
or better still, an "august seismograph
whose charts we haven't the training to read."
    Another critic (whose work did in fact
receive a chapter in *Axel's Castle*)
would not concede even this much. "If [Stein]
is of the future," he wrote in his review
of *Composition as Explanation*,
 "then the future is, as it very likely
sis, of the barbarians." He would not
have been wrong had he written: *of the bots.*

[24] Née Harvard Annex. The local clinical
context for Solomons' and Stein's paper
is "that most interesting phenomenon"
then known as "double personality"
which was exhibited, in extreme cases,
by patients then known as "hysterical

By several decades,[25] not to mention
The jump it got on current research into
The attention economies of our
Era of information overload;[26]
That 2. The apartment (address: 27
Rue de Fleurus) she shares, at first, with her
Brother Leo, and then with her life-partner
Alice B. Toklas, is *the central node*
In one of the densest artistic networks
Ever configured, one that regulated
The passage of nearly every writer
Considered above, as well as that of
A rising generation of expat
Popularizers whom she was to tutor,
Fall out with, and finally label 'lost,'
Though none meant more to her than the painters
She and Leo collected, promoted,

subjects." The two students set out to see,
as their title suggests, whether "essential
elements" of the so-called disorder
could be reproduced under artificial
conditions in a "normal," i.e., non-
hysterical subject, viz., Gertrude Stein.

[25] In the lab, experiments were performed
on Stein that would not have been out of place
at a séance. But then *ein Medium
ist ein Medium ist ein Medium*,
as Kittler's tongue, snugly in cheek, remarks.

[26] "Normal Motor Automatism" concludes
that "whatever else hysteria may be . . .
[i]t is a *disease* of the *attention*,"
a judgment which, as anyone who looks
up from this footnote to the nearest screen
(unless you are already reading it
on one) can attest, has aged far better
than the famed study of the disorder
that came out the year before in Vienna.
    "Everybody," as she was to observe
in *Wars I Have Seen*, her last published text,
"gets so much information all day long
that they lose their common sense." Paul Stevens,
who uses this quote as the epigraph
of *The Poetics of Information
Overload*, which casts Stein as the godmother
of experimental writing, also
quotes a 2008 UCSD
study which estimates that "the average
American 'consume[s]' 100,000
words per day" a statistic which, a dozen
years later, is already out of date.

Or sat for (while Alice sat with their wives)
And whose technical breakthroughs on canvas
She would ingeniously transpose to the page,
From her early post-impressionist 'portraits,'
To *Tender Buttons'* 'verbal cubist' still lifes,
To the nonrepresentational *Stanzas*
In Meditation,[27] which would mark the end
Of her experimental period,
A career arc[28] that definitively
Redefines language's relationship
To the visual arts for a number
Of later schools of avant-garde poetry;[29]
And that 3. By beginning with the sentence
Rather than the word, selecting grammar
As the philosophical problem she
Would grapple with, rather than reference,
As soberer minds than Marinetti
And Tzara (e.g., Russell, Wittgenstein)

[27] A "long dull poem" à la "Wordsworth and Crabbe"
was how Stein herself described the project
in her correspondence with Lindley Hubbell.
Qtd. in Retallack's introduction
("On Not Not Reading . . .") to the Yale edition.

[28] The presentation of which selectively
excludes her contributions to other
genres: fiction, theater, criticism:
though such categories no longer seem
adequate to properly describe her work.

[29] In his 1957 review
of the posthumously published *Stanzas*,
the future author of the Horatian
"And *Ut Pictura Poesis* Is Her Name"
compared the book, with one eye on his own
practice, to a "monochrome by de Kooning,"
which again puts Stein, w/r/t trans-
media influence, ahead of her time.
    The reviewer, of course, was soon to become
a member of the so-called New York School,
modeled after the informal name given
to the abstract expressionist painters
(like de Kooning) they admired. With a few
notable exceptions, e.g., OuLiPo
(mathematics) and Language Poetry
(lit crit.)—though the 'co-optees' and 'colleagues'
of both of these movements would acknowledge
the influence of other parts of Stein's *oeuvre*
on their work—the visual arts will be
a primary source of inspiration
for the Noigandres Group, the Black Mountain School,

Were doing, combined with her *stuplime*[30] flood
Of paratactic fragments and run-ons,
And the permutational activation
Of other grammatical potentials
Which were less forbidden by semantics
Than they were those regions of linguistic
Infrastructure operating below
The threshold of meaning (considered as use),
Stein *drowns* the syntax that Marinetti
Had failed to destroy through decimation,
Giving literature—as opposed to
Psychiatry—its first glimpse at what occurs,
In Barthes' notorious paraphrase, when
C'est le langage qui parle [et] pas l'auteur.
    Now do you agree? Anyhow. *Q.E.D.*

the Lettrists and the Situationists,
Fluxus poets, conceptual poets,
and the found, Flarf, and digital poetries
of the early 21st century.

[30] A portmanteau of *stupid* and *sublime*
coined by Sianne Ngai to capture the affect
of shock-boredom astonishment-fatigue
that is produced by the "'thick' language" of
so much modern and postmodern writing.
Following Gilles Deleuze, Ngai attributes
this "ugly feeling" to the "exchange of
formal differences for modal" ones,
to a "relentlessly materialist
environment of words" where coherence
"operates as a vast combinatory"
and, finally, to the logic of the Law
of Large Numbers, which invades and exhausts
syntactic conventions, esp.
the ones that govern the representation
of causality and temporal sequence,
i.e., the motors of hypotaxis.

KURT LUCHS

ALL ABOARD! D. H. LAWRENCE AND "THE SHIP OF DEATH"

D. H. LAWRENCE'S poetic reputation has forever been overshadowed by his fame as a fiction writer, much like Thomas Hardy before him (though not all that much before him; it's odd to reflect that Hardy died in 1928, only two years before Lawrence, and that the bulk of Hardy's poetic production was contemporaneous with that of Lawrence, his junior by 45 years). Yet I have always felt that his poems are superior to even the best of his novels, which of course are quite good, except for the ghastly *Lady Chatterley's Lover*.

Further, Lawrence's career as a poet prefigures those of some of the most talented poets in England and America several generations after him. I'm thinking of Ted Hughes, Sylvia Plath, James Wright, W. S. Merwin and Donald Hall, among others. Like Lawrence, each of these poets began by writing formal verse and then, compelled by the lure of new themes and new ways of thinking, as well as the spirit of the times, switched to free verse. In every case this change raised their work to a new level. The curious thing about Lawrence is that the transition from rhymes to free verse did not so much result in better work—he wrote great poems in both styles—but rather it was part of his lifelong quest to become ever more his true self, free of constraints and preconceptions.

Lawrence's journey of self-discovery ran parallel to his work and was fascinating both to him and to his friends and enemies. As Aldous Huxley noted, "Isn't it remarkable how everyone who knew Lawrence felt compelled to write about him?" Huxley's roman à clef *Point Counter Point* contains a character based on Lawrence, the fiery writer-artist-social critic Mark Rampion, and *Brave New World* is in many ways a reaction to the denatured dystopia that Huxley and Lawrence saw the world becoming.

"The Ship of Death" is certainly one of Lawrence's best poems, as well as the most famous. Not every writer knows when death is coming and has time and vitality enough to ponder it fruitfully. After years of suffering from tuberculosis, Lawrence finally began to succumb to it in the late 1920s. Before he died on March 2, 1930, he had given death a thorough going-over in a number of poems, most memorably in "Bavarian Gentians" and "The Ship of Death."

The latter poem is almost unique among poetic masterpieces in that it has no definitive version. While he had toiled through multiple drafts, some of them published separately, and the last version is the most complete, it is clearly unfinished. For example, in the beginning of the poem he starts some sentences with the poetic apostrophe "O," but at the middle and end he slips into the more workaday "Oh" for no apparent reason. Surely this minor inconsistency would've been cleaned up if he had lived.

That there is no definitive text of "The Ship of Death" may not matter as much as you might think, for several reasons. For one thing, though Lawrence was not a slapdash writer, he was also not a persnickety perfectionist, at least not in the sense of the poem as well-wrought-urn (see: Cleanth Brooks). As death approached, his idea of perfection had more to do with imaginative liberty and spontaneity, with capturing the moment. Then, too, this poem is about a journey into the unknown. It is in its nature to be open-ended and partially undefined.

The poem can be read as a liturgy for the dying, not unlike the *Tibetan Book of the Dead* or certain passages in the *Anglican Book of Common Prayer*. There are ten stanzas of varying lengths, each one a poem in its own right, and altogether adding up to something much more than the sum of its parts. In "The Ship of Death" as in nearly all of Lawrence's better free verse poems, the main poetic influence is not any of his predecessors or contemporaries. It is the King James Bible, especially the most explicitly poetic part of it, the Psalms. His sonorities, his imagery, and most of all his artful use of reiteration has its roots there.

Stanza I sets the scene and makes the autumnal mood official by using falling apples as a metaphor for death:

> Now it is autumn and the falling fruit
> and the long journey towards oblivion.

Already we can discern that this poem about death will be neither overly morbid nor sad. In fact, as we will see, despite some dark passages it is downright joyful. From the start he is treating death as part of the natural order. What's more, the death of a lone apple seems less tragic in that the tree from which it fell, the greater life, continues.

Stanza II brings the ship of death into it, although we have little idea at this point what the ship might be. Not a literal ship, at any rate, as it would be if the poem were two or three thousand years old and written about the death of a king instead of a modern everyman.

In Stanza III Lawrence takes a step sideways to deal with the issue of suicide. On the whole, he seems to be against it, "for how could murder, even self-murder / ever a quietus make?" It's worth noting that the author spent years dying from one of the most insidious diseases imaginable, but did not take his own life. No matter how painful, he viewed the death journey as sacrosanct, an essential human experience, not something to be dodged. The goal, he says in Stanza IV, is "a strong heart at peace." And here, I think, is his conception of the ship of death—a mental construct, a deep feeling, a final alignment of the best part of the inner person.

This theme becomes more explicit in Stanza V, where he speaks of "the long and painful death / that lies between the old self and the new." That almost sounds like the Christian notion of death, yet he is careful in his verse, just as he was in his life, not to affiliate himself with any one tradition, preferring to borrow from them all to make his own. And when in the same stanza he writes, "Already the dark and endless ocean of the end / is washing in through the breaches of your wounds," it is a strangely inverted echo of the crucifixion, where instead of the wounds bleeding out, the waters of death bleed in through them. Very peculiar, and very much Lawrence.

Stanza VI is about the individual's fear of death, and also mentions his belief that human civilization is destroying itself in a collective death. The word is still out on that prophecy, though performing gain-of-function research on a deadly virus can't be a good sign.

Death finally comes for the Archbishop Lawrence in Stanza VII, and he says of the ship of death:

> She is gone! gone! and yet
> somewhere she is there.
> Nowhere!

The end? Not quite. While Stanza VIII affirms, "It is the end, it is oblivion," Stanza IX witnesses some kind of rebirth, "the cruel dawn of coming back to life / out of oblivion," and concludes with, "A flush of rose, and the whole thing starts again." That certainly appears to be an allusion to reincarnation. Once again, however, it would be hasty to attribute this to belief in anything as specific as Hinduism or Buddhism.

Stanza X reiterates the image of rebirth and finishes with a rousing exhortation nearly identical to the one that begins Stanza II:

Oh build your ship of death, oh build it!
for you will need it.
For the voyage of oblivion awaits you.

Lawrence's ship of death metaphor is not quite like any other. It is not a ship set aflame to bury a Viking at sea, nor is it the boat in which Charon ferries the dead across the River Styx (or was that the River REO Speedwagon?). Like everything else he wrote, it is unique to him, and like the best of his work, it achieves universality. It started as his ship of death, but it's ours now. As Kenneth Rexroth writes in his Introduction to the *Selected Poems* published by New Directions, "*The Ship of Death* poems have an exaltation, a nobility, a steadiness, an insouciance, which is not only not of this time but which is rare in any time." Incidentally, though that volume is out of print, it's worth tracking down used, both for the quality of the selection and for Rexroth's essay, one of the best ever written about Lawrence.

Kurt Luchs

The Canoe of Death

(With no apologies and a taffy apple to D.H. Lawrence.)

I.
Now it is Fall and the falling fruit
falls on me and sends me on the long journey towards oblivion.

Like swollen balls of dew they fall
down my shirt and briefs and seem to say, "No exit,"
but Jean-Paul Sartre used that already
and what is he but a fallen fruit?
Perhaps it is Springtime instead?
Anyway, it is time to look in the mirror
and wave bye-bye at one's self. So long!

II.
Have you carved your canoe of death, O tell me have you?
O you must carve your canoe of death,
I insist, really you must,
for they come in ever so handy when you are dead.
I've ridden in mine countless times.

But now Suzie Snowflake is nipping at my nose.
Was that thunder I heard, or . . . No, it was just another
apple that fell on my head. Silly me!
And death is on the air like an old cardigan sweater.
Dear me, can't you smell that nasty smell?
Someone is burning leaves.
And in the bruised apple, yes, the very same one
I told you about, the little worm is wriggling.
How tiny and cold he is!
There's a lesson there, don't you think?

III.

Quiet, please, O I beg you be quiet,
I can't hear myself think, it's such a tiny sound
like a dagger bruising a bare bodkin
or a bullet being bitten, O don't you see?
If you don't shut up I shall murder you. Ah!

IV.

(A minute of silence.)

V.

So build your canoe of death, you'll need it
where you're going, bye-bye, far away
where the sugar plums grow and never fall
nasty plop! on your head and make it all sticky
like a slimy nasty old worm. Ugh! O ugh I say!
Already something has soaked my breeches,
the waters of the infinite sea of boredom
are drenching my codpiece.

O carve your canoe of death, you witless twit,
stock it with tuna fish salad and candied apples
and powdered milk and sugarless gum—*anything*,
just so you go away
and don't come back.

VI.

We are dying, O please let us die dear God,
I won't forgive you if you don't
for we are dying bit by bit,
our noses are falling off,
I feel dead already, don't you?
O say that you do!

VII.

(A minute of quiet, bitter sobbing.)

VIII.

*(Several minutes of uncontrolled weeping, followed by
the Author falling to his hands and knees
and banging his head on the floor.)*

IX.

(The sobbing gradually becomes a violent, hacking cough.)

X.

Let us sail our little canoe through the lagoon of life,
Let's see if we can sink it, shall we?
O dear God the doctor says I will live after all!
I threw an apple at him and he bruised beautifully.
Then he smiled and sank my boats in the bathtub.
I could have kissed him for joy.
But instead I held him under the suds
and started him on the long journey towards oblivion.

Thomas Walton

Unsavory Thoughts

Jesus Was a Thrasher

MY DAUGHTER and I were staring at the painting for a while. Not because it was a great painting, it wasn't, but because we were tired. We'd been at the museum for a few hours already. They didn't have a café. We were exhausted, so we found an empty bench and sat down. The bench just happened to be placed in front of the painting we were staring at.

"It would be better," I said, "if they put the benches by windows, or in front of a black wall, so you could take a break from looking."

But the bench was in front of the painting, a nativity scene. I didn't recognize the artist. The baby, Christ, was on some blankets on the ground. He had his hands up, as if to push Mary away. Joseph was in the background, near a barn. Joseph was also looking at the baby, everyone was, even the donkey and the chickens seemed to be eyeing the child. But the baby, weirdly, didn't seem very happy, didn't seem very "Christ-like." A beam of sunlight illuminated the fat rolls on his arms and legs.

"It's weird that Jesus is always a baby," my daughter said. She's 15, no longer a baby. "Why wouldn't God just make him a man? Why did he have to make him a baby first?"

"No idea," I said.

"Like Jesus had to go to school, and be a teenager, and do homework . . . "

I shook my head.

"Do you think he played an instrument?" she said.

"No idea," I said, and looked around to see if anyone could hear us, "you mean like the saxophone?"

My daughter played the saxophone, mostly when I forced her to practice. "Yeah."

"Don't know," I said, "but I think your projecting a little bit. Do you have a Jesus complex or something?"

"No," she said. We were quiet for a few minutes. Both of us went on staring at the painting. "It is weird to think of him as a teenager, though." she laughed, "He looks weird. He's so white, and fat. And even though he's a baby, his face looks like a man's face."

I shook my head and looked around again. No one was near us. "I feel like I should point out that that's not Jesus, it's just a rendering of Jesus."

"I bet Jesus was one of the popular kids," she said.

"You mean like in the lunchroom?"

"Yeah. I bet he was a skater . . . "

"Don't know," I said, "I haven't seen any paintings of Jesus at a skate park."

"Yeah . . . why is he always a baby? Or dead? Or eating dinner?"

"Don't know."

". . . and why are the angels always in the background? And nobody seems to notice? If there were angels in real life everyone would be like 'oh my god look there's some angels on the roof of the barn,' and everyone would look at them. They wouldn't just ignore them like 'oh yeah, there's those fucking angels on the roof of the barn again.'"

"Hey . . . "

"What?"

"Don't say 'fucking'."

"You say it."

"I know but . . . not about angels."

We looked at the painting for a few more minutes. And then she said, "Every museum should have a fucking café."

Are You Flossing?

"READING'S A WASTE of time," the dental hygienist said, hands in blue rubber gloves, blue rubber gloves in my mouth. "I like documentaries, though. I'm watching one now on the Challenger Space Craft. Remember that?"

"mmhmm."

"Open," she said, and filled my mouth with water. "Close." I closed, and the vacuum tube sucked all the water and saliva out of my mouth. "Open." she said, and the blue rubber gloves dove back in.

". . . a book, though, I don't know, sometimes when I'm reading a book I feel like my life is just passing me by. It's kind of a waste of time. Turn."

I turned.

"Good. I read one book recently about some farmers or something. I don't even know what was going on. They were on a machine, a tractor I guess. Turn your head to the side a little. Good. There were about eight of them on this tractor . . ."

"hmm"

". . . I know right. It was weird. Open. I think it was digging potatoes somehow, a potato harvester I guess, I don't know. Close."

I closed, and the vacuum did its thing again.

"It was the weirdest story. Open. There was a fight between two of the farmers. I guess farmers isn't the right word. They were like itinerant workers, I guess. Not Mexicans, though. Okay put your head straight again. They were white, I guess. Oh you're bleeding. Are you flossing?"

"mmm . . ."

"You really need to floss every night."

"umhmm."

"I love Mexican food, though. You like Mexican food?"

"mmm"

"My favorite are those fajitas. I think that's so fun the way they serve them on those iron skillets you know?"

"mmm"

"all sizzling there at the table, it's so fun . . . but margaritas are too sweet for me. My husband will drink two or three but I just have a Seven-up. If he has three I have to drive. Close. Good. How we doin?"

"Good."

"Good, now let's turn your head to the side a bit again right there, almost done . . . He says tequila is his weakness . . . huh! tequila and any other alcohol. You know what I mean?"

"umhmm."

"But I guess we all have our weaknesses. Mine's documentaries. I could watch documentaries for hours. The History Channel. I love history. The one on the Challenger Space Shuttle was real good . . . you know they knew right?"

"hmm?"

"They knew. The O rings were . . . well they knew the O rings would fail."

She took her hands out of my mouth and I took a deep breath.

"Okay?" she asked.

"Yes." I took another deep breath and she threw her hands back into my mouth.

"I guess it was the engineers. They tried to tell the, the officials you know, of the, of the launch I guess, but they wouldn't believe them."

"hmm."

"Yeah, I wasn't clear exactly who knew what but they knew that the O rings would fail. Open wide now. Those poor astronauts."

"mmm."

"It's one of those things where you remember where you were, you know?"

"mmm."

"I was a freshman in high school. I didn't like high school very much. Okay let's rinse you out now . . . and close." She put the vacuum in and sucked out all the water. "Okay, almost done. Turn just a . . . perfect. I think they had it on in my Social Studies class, and everyone . . . I'm gonna have you close your mouth just a little bit. Right there. Great. Everyone just gasped like 'oh no'"

"mmm"

"The way the spaceship just exploded out of nowhere . . . "

"mmm"

"Those poor astronauts."

"mmm"

"All those bits of burnt bodies all flying through space and sizzling, melted skin and faces and everything"

"hmm"

"It was so horrible."

"mmhmm"

"I would've loved to see the expression on their faces when they knew they were about to burn to death."

"hm?"

"Close. Good . . . but books. I don't know. A book is too much to suffer through. I'd much rather watch something."

Go Find Your Brother

WHEN WE were kids, my brother and I wrapped duct tape around whiffle balls and threw them at each other, trying to hit each other in the face. Oh sure, we started out playing a proper whiffle ball game, but the game always devolved into war. And tears.

My brother had no sense of the ethics of war. He feigned ignorance of the Geneva Convention, or any other convention for that matter. War crimes to him were not taboo, but exercises in innovation. He threw all kinds of things at me—whiffle balls, baseball bats, skateboards, hammers. He put the gorilla in guerilla warfare: in fact, if he'd had a gorilla he would've thrown it at me.

Every whiffle ball contest (now that I think of it, every contest of any kind) ended with him running into the garage and searching for something to launch at me. He usually missed. I was agile enough to avoid his attempts. Besides, it's surprisingly easy to dodge a hatchet thrown at you by a hysterical seven-year-old. Even if you are only nine.

He did connect on occasion, and I still have a few scars as evidence of his success. Once, an aluminum baseball bat spinning wildly through the air caught me in the knee. It didn't hurt so much as tingle, like when you hit your funny bone on something.

The worst was the hubcap. The hubcap came whizzing toward me like a UFO, except that I knew the whole time that it was a hubcap. It was an IFO. I ran when I saw it coming, zig zagging to try to avoid its trajectory, but its coordinates were somehow locked in on me and it caught me on the crown of my head. I fell, and then put my hand up to my head. I could feel the warm blood trickling down the back of my neck. There was a gash in my head, and a thick flap of skin had flipped up and filled with hair. It burned and bled and beat like a throbbing drum.

That's the time, after the hubcap, that I'd had enough. I confess I beat him to a pulp. I confess I derived a kind of sadistic pleasure from it. I confess that after the beating, I stuffed him in one of those garbage bins that latch shut. I confess that I told him if he made a single sound, I would roll the garbage can into the hole where we dumped all the rotten apples and grass clippings, and we both knew was full of snakes and spiders and hornet nests.

"You better not make a sound," I said, and went inside.

An hour or so later, at dinner, we all sat down and started eating. My parents, my two older sisters and me.

"Where's your brother?" my dad said, with a tired expression.

I shrugged, "don't know."

He turned his head away from the TV to look at me, "Go find him."

I went out to the garbage bin. There must've been holes in it, because he was still alive. I unlatched the lid and opened it. He was trembling slightly, and there were dirt streaks under his eyes where the tears had run.

"Dinner's ready."

BOBBY PARROTT

TO REMOVE THE BATTERIES, PULL THE LEVER MARKED *OPEN*

WHEN YOU remove the batteries from my Orphic Accordion, its metal reeds fall into a reverse euphoria, blur of motion disengaged like trained circus kazoos on holiday. We smile aloud. Radiant frogs low in the gullies, we eclipse facsimile in our bloated blurps. Our nictitating membranes thicken to astral, and we lounge in our buttoned-up dugouts half asleep. But can we sustain this breach, this empty? Dare we mimic the pearloid mantle of a thrice-erupted volcano, translucent as taste?

Dante would. Impelled by the strict birds of fortuity, he's hopscotched executive contradictions of his own, dialectics thrown into retrospect. From our tiny portholes we candle ideas of liquefaction, aspects of a broken astronomy gone lucid. The way constellations clockwork the years, their calibration of arcs across this packet of black. *Life, a miniature version—a trickle immersion,* I tell myself, lulled by the swings and tilts of my Speed Graphic. In its Cyclops box, one glass eye mounted in metal rings, f-stop dilated to subjugate thumbs into scrubbish big toes.

These digits of discontent separated from birth. Get them close. Introductions will not be necessary. Together, can they fix the disconnect? Seem nightly the squid of thorax? I know not *seem,* though we moisturize our brains with drippings from other squeamish complexities, yawn to bursting. Like the oyster dredged as he harbors clarity in a pearl that has yet to transmit light. The way the lens in a frog's eye pulls faint starlight in like a radio signal. Must we delay this protoplasmic fusion by sipping Chardonnay from monosyllabic flutes? Which reminds me: Moonlight in taillights. The rubbery heads of mushrooms, rubbing hard and on our side. Synthesized in the grassy manure of gods, we clutch armless and discharged this erasable plane of afraid.

Russell Bennetts

Three Poems

Greeted as Liberators

Photons almost lonely for mattress fumes pointed eastward.
Eastwood scene for mountain-grabbled crashgallop.
Tree asplintered for further cavalier grace.
Only when Death's Hotel gets signal can sworn
varnish kick bottled openings.

Foolish Miracles

speedboat stoners washed shuttered sidewalked
rocking fairground, rocking fairground
those yellow stairs boosted
towering cacti

sand response red shine
from the state of hyper-tense past state of realty

narrowed prosperity
tested rides
smokedup burger shot

counter-educated hung
distilled union depositary
flowed one-time media shown
ever-bulled rocked muck of reality's bear appetite

pan-club goods refuelled alongside LA's kicker
motorsport's deluxe premium sweated and spilled

spilt rum
pills:tragedy

clubs clubs discoteques
wrecked eyelids
translated between lines
warrior star sold soul constraint wine-ether
younger than me

electric fountains

closured hoochholes marvels
the pace of change the pace of change
wallowed midlands
then the sweats game

WE BELIEVE

IN OUR

PURPLE TIGERS

Creator's airport over Albion's tasted press bone broth sinewed, an opened casket kinda Tuesday each month passed employed cyberpunked sessions curiously enough, an over-engineered energy drink ban blue moon ain't *our* life, no turning regenerate to improve your drinking stats with handstands, hatstands and crashes City Paints. Inc. out smoking diddly dose another gnarly branch 100% completion Motel rising as the sun burns off fogged palms who is the ultimate sugared benefactor? deustche cooking predicated on rap comics double-fisted mourning coffee while stationary whilst stationed at Yoshi's successful, money-making sushi franchise enterprise impactful rage dreams of slower drank cash, shifted racing-wise ever-rookie street racer, point-to-point pier-to-pier sulphurous consecrated grounds shining silver, cascading, shaded Her hollowed, nuked aspersions to bubbling chambers a social buccaneer, enormous in Dublin doubtless, doubled blues himself contained within faded opera delivered ranch undressings and accumulated grime we're mudmen, sprung with straw phone off, unplugged glitter glitter unplugged, esteemed as foul foiled Nero's hallways still: powdered coffee power!

J.A. Tyler

Children's Games for the Apocalypse

How to Play Blood Gnats

FOLLOW THEM with your eyes, their patterns the erratic same, hovering like dust motes before they loop and swerve. Follow them through the varied backgrounds: the stained carpets, the rubble, the damp walls. Follow them until you have one in sight, then clap your hands. Slowly—slowly—undo your palms. If they are empty, the same dry skin under blue-mooned light, you've lost. If you have the smear of a gnat somewhere in the creases of your fingers, you're closer, though a smear is only a placeholder. You haven't won until you see a blooded slash on your hands, burgeoning from a gnarled body.

How to Play Seek & Hiding

Wrap your arms around a loved one. Squeeze tight. When all is wrung, close your eyes and walk slowly away from one another. Back away like the other is a polar magnet, an opposite, a star collapsing. Back away with definitive steps. Back away, eyes closed, until you've receded like a wave into the ocean, like a cloud in a sky gone dark, blue-lit by an erroring moon, by the lack of everything that once was. When you and your loved one have truly lost one another inside this rupturing, open your eyes. The game, from then on, is to seek one another while always backing away.

How to Play Grass Hunt

Kneel down. Get on all fours and prowl slow, like a water buffalo. Walk in twosomes like the hitched steps of an electric-drunk. Pick a gait. Stick to it. If you're moving like a kangaroo, move like a kangaroo. If you've chosen the lope of a cow, lope. The grace and mindfulness of a horse, go. The game is about the movements. You should feel your muscles stretch, your tendons pull. Then, in your animal poses, in your otherwise glances, search for the grass. Search for the lost meadow, the gone fields. Search for any green blade, any plant growing by itself. Search for a slip of real vegetation. If you find grass—real grass—the game is over.

How to Play Nightmare

Think about when the lights went out. Think about how the world went dark, every ounce of electricity vanquished. Pretend you're there, on that night. Pretend you're holding a candle. Pretend you're cradling a flashlight, praying the batteries don't die. Pretend you're only hoping to survive. Think of the blood. Think about the blue-quiet of jet fuel burning, of lights and sirens receding, a landscape quilted with the moans of the dying. Pretend you're digging through the collapse. Pretend you're holding your breath for fear of the air. Pretend you're leading a lost child back to its mother. Now, pretend the mother is dead. Pretend the family across the street has vanished. Pretend the TVs will never come back on. Pretend so hard that you implode.

How to Play Survival

Hold still forever. Or wait until everyone quits screaming. Or run until your breath is exhausted, or until someone catches you, whichever comes first. Or move as slowly as possible, so slowly that you might be mistaken for a passing cloud. Burst each part of yourself in the hopes that no one will find you tomorrow. Or chase down someone else, run, tackle them, and steal their heart.

How to Play Blindness

Stare at the blue moon until it hurts. Stare past the hurt. Stare until blue becomes less a color than a feeling. Stare until there is no blue anymore and the world dims. Stare until the sky begins to curl. When this happens, immediately close your eyes. Snap them shut and pray. The words are unimportant. What you're really doing, behind closed eyes, is holding until a message appears on the inside of your eyelids. Wait long enough and it will show itself in an electric swirl, loosening on the dark canvas. To end the game, simply open your eyes.

How to Play Separation Anxiety

Find a partner. Face each other and hold hands. If you're missing a hand, do your best. If you're missing both hands, use the stump ends where your hands used to be. Look into your partner's eyes and imagine a world without them. Imagine those thousands of planes careening down from the sky. When it feels like everything will collapse, let go and walk away. Go. Move so far away that you don't exist anymore. Until your partner doesn't remember you. Never come back.

How to Play Burning

A player counts to one hundred. As soon as they begin counting, start packing your existence onto your back. Be sure to take not just the jewelry and keepsakes but the way the home smells and tastes and feels. Pack the memories into your mouth. Pack the sentiments through your chest. Be sure to cross the burning threshold before the other player reaches one hundred.

How to Play Looking for Love

Ask another player to soak the carpet in kerosene and light the drapes on fire. If you don't have drapes, use the walls. Stand there until everything burns around you. Stand there until nothing is left. Stand there until you disintegrate.

How to Play Memory Eraser

Find a pocket of warm wind. Sit in it, holding your breath. Try to ignore the piles of greened bricks or the leafless trunks of dead saplings, the nearby beams of moonlight. When you are ready, take a deep breath. After the inhale, try to remember what you were doing there in the first place. If you can recall what the game was, you win. Play until everyone forgets.

How to Play Dead as a Doornail

First, arrange yourselves in pairs. One of each pair plays dead. Go limp or slump chairside or slit your own throat. The mode and manner of deadening is wide open. When one partner is dead, the other must go on living half as if nothing happened. Eat. Sleep. Travel. Talk. Go on without hesitation, sustaining it for as long as possible. The game ends when either the dead refuses to stay dead or the living can't go on.

How to Play Pretend You're Something You're Not

Stand somewhere. The middle of a stark field. A broken street. Some half-charred living room. Stand and imagine as far away from yourself as possible. When your imagination is really humming, start telling everyone about the new you, the you this burned-down world has made. Keep telling them until you believe it, way inside, untouchable and frank. Keep telling it until it becomes inseparable from the you that once was. Keep playing until the moon falls from the sky, until the world is no longer a world you know.

How to Play A Candle in the Window

Go into hiding. Find a house to live in. Arrange the furniture and decorate the walls. Put a candle in the window. Swing the door shut and pretend away the explosions and the pallor of your face, the chaos dotting your eyes. Melt into what once was. Make a new kind of living built entirely from a scattered, ugly history.

How to Play Unbecoming

Spread ten players out on ten tables in a room as blank as canvas and ceilin- gless, all ten looking up at the stars. Listen to a morning full of birds piped through the walls. Strip naked in the perpetual cool of the blue-hewn air, hearts slowing to a murmur. Then one additional player will bring out a knife, dragging it methodically across those ten throats, blood steaming in the dark. The last one to remain prostrate amid the sunless sky and the birds and the blood, unbecomes.

How to Play Bloom

Three players stand in a line, arms linked, and walk down the deserted highways, walking until the land turns to nothingness. The three players then sit together and play that antique game, Paper Rock Scissors. The winner of it stands, raising hands to the sky. The other two will wield blades and flay the skin from the winner, whittling until the body is bright and lively again, until all of them  have bloomed.

Nate Logan

The Good Life

December

The kids each brought home a cannibalistic holiday wreath. Immediately we thought of Elvis's biggest fan, his plastic fangs. We hung a monstrosity on each door. A grim view of Indianapolis nightlife is what the book sales rep wanted to keep intact—that's what she said, anyway. "I appreciate your dedication, but I've already selected my books for the semester," I said. Pizza was delivered. A mom on screen was attacked by something in the tinsel.

No One Asked

The eyes of 1979 belong to Meg Foster; I'm sorry, I don't make the rules. The TV psychic was brought in because how much could it hurt. No one's gonna tell me I have to give up my landline phone. At brunch, someone at the next table says something now has a "life of its own." That's usually when the rug gets pulled out, the other loafer drops, etc. When I got to my car, it was enrobed in confetti. It's not my birthday.

Woof

When I return from the department meeting, a telegram on my desk: LIVE THE GOOD LIFE IN VULCANOLOGY.

Erin had a knack for putting the pieces together. Her voice adopted a serious timbre when showing guests nudie puzzles above the fireplace and dog bowl.

Buzz, your girlfriend. Buzz, tiny sparrows flew right by your bird condo.

Seeing all the epigraphs side by side, a theme emerged.

I power walked from the library, a clue with your name on it tucked in my front pocket.

We can agree: the horror workout video was not the Steely Dan of the genre, as much as we would've loved it.

If you don't get a bike helmet to go with your new wheels, you're going to hear about it.

"Helium comes from radioactive decay of elements with half lives in the billions of years and we piss it away filling the boss baby."

Throwing back almonds in the laboratory, thinking about needing to get more almonds.

On another plane. I still got my mind set on you.

CHWEN-YUEN ANGIE CHEN

Damage

I N THE WORLD of Pokémon, damage is a complex calculation that seems to be debated endlessly by Pokémon players. Most damages outside of direct hits involve a complex formula that looks something like this:

$$Damage = \left(\frac{\left(\frac{2 \times Level}{5} + 2 \right) \times Power \times A/D}{50} + 2 \right) \times Modifier$$

Modifiers depend on many variables including "weather, effectiveness of attack, the type of injury, whether burn, water, heat, *astonishment*, body slam, earthquake, or *shadow force…*"

As you can see, modifiers can alter the magnitude of damage with a large range of results, outside of those non-modifiable factors that make you who you are. I suppose humans are like this too, and I wonder about all the kinds of modifiers that are out of our control that knock us around day after day, then year after year, leaving gashes like the marks left on sharks or whales from territorial skirmishes or contests over scarcity of food and mates—these injuries are permanent identifiers, redefining who they are, so distinctive that one can tell an individual shark from another just by the markings of their *damage*.

I wonder about *damage*; the calculations that make up our collective versus individual damage. *Your* damage is not contained in a vacuum. It leaks and can become part of *my* calculus of damage. I wonder about my personal damage, and the cost it has levied. I wonder about others' damage and why it's hidden so well, or perhaps, not. Raw *damage* can lack compassion, and empathy; it enables one to be cruel and exact revenge. But there are times when *damage* transforms into the

gift of clairvoyance because *damage* learns the unspoken language of body and facial expressions. You become a master of "reading the room."

E MIL* WAS 24 when he was referred to my addiction medicine practice after hearing about me from his primary care doctor who tried preventing his return to heroin use by prescribing buprenorphine. He looked 30 years late for a Cyndi Lauper concert with tightly-fitting, low-riding black denims, a studded black leather jacket, an asymmetric haircut, wearing a dog collar around his neck and smelling of patchouli. That appointment visit was on 9/11 and the irony of the tragic anniversary date was not lost upon us. As I sat down beside him at the computer console, I think I made a good first impression by mentioning dispassionately, "I used to work on the 89th floor of the North Tower, had to walk down those staircases once for a fire alarm. Took forever. Must have been a truly fucked-up thing trying to escape that day . . ." as I scrolled through his electronic medical record.

"Holy shit. . ." I heard him whisper. I could sense him trying to size me up.

Still remaining fixed on the screen and scrolling, I pursed my lips downward, raised my eyebrows and nodded in agreement. Then I turned to him. "Emil. Hi. Really glad you're here." I let out an audible exhalation and smiled. I meant it. I was really glad he was there. He had recently suffered another DUI, spent a night in jail, and was debating whether to leave for his fifth or sixth residential drug and alcohol treatment center.

"Doc? Listen, I want a comfortable detox with phenobarbital, I'm pretty sure I have PAWS, and I'm really scared that I can't stop this potent benzo

* "Emil" is not his real name, and people and events around him have been altered to protect his identity.

shit I'm getting online. Which I haven't told anyone. What do you think about high dose fish oil?"

"High dose fish oil?" (Yes, you just had the same reaction I did.)

"I basically paid $700 for about 20 minutes of some asshole's time who didn't understand my history. He recommended fish oil."

"Who has you on phenobarb?"

"No one!" He shot me a look like I was a dimwit. "I *want* phenobarb to get off this flubromazolam. I take about three—four—five drops of that crap at a time, I can't get off, but I'm a shitty sleeper—have been all my life."

He was right to be annoyed, I hadn't been listening. I was still stuck on "high dose fish oil."

Emil called himself a "garbage head," but the less pejorative terminology is "having polysubstance use disorder." He started smoking tobacco and drinking alcohol heavily by 13. He was currently using intravenous crystal methamphetamine, and smoking cannabis; he was prescribed Adderall, buprenorphine, clonazepam, gabapentin, quetiapine, aripiprazole, and flurazepam, and he had dabbled with LSD, DMT, heroin, inhalants, and an illicit designer benzodiazepine, flubromazolam, which was only available on the internet.

What kind of *damage* causes a highly intelligent university student—whose immigrant father was a political dissident author, and whose mother was a PhD chemist — to need to self-medicate with substances that would have most obtunded for days?

Over time, Emil described how his father routinely and violently disturbed his sleep to interrogate and belittle him, keeping Emil awake for hours and usually for no discernable reason. He got through high school, somehow, and made it to college. It was no mystery why he slept poorly, had nightmares, and sought escape in a myriad of ways as an adolescent. Under my care, Emil would intermittently return to harmful drug use. He attempted to re-enroll in school which became a stressor he couldn't withstand. He would be with friends who used drugs and drank, and he couldn't resist. Every relationship that ruptured would transport him to the painful memory of losing the love of his life to a drug overdose. Every stressor seemed intolerable. This is what Dr. George Koob, addiction neurobiologist, coined as hyperkatifeia: a hypersensitivity to emotional distress in the context of opioid use disorder. For Emil, and so many of us, it was most likely a hypersensitivity that was initially caused by *damage*.

Emil looked at me one day and cried, "I don't think you get it . . . I wish you knew how it feels . . ."

I T'S BEEN A LONG WHILE since I have felt damaged, which is something separate from *being* damaged, yet there was a time I felt terribly damaged. Damaged enough to hurt myself with acts of self-mutilation, alcohol, and drugs, with forced purging and depression too deep to even have the energy left to want relief. *Damage* can look like avoidant behavior, when there is not enough psychological real estate for the needs of other people. Avoidance of emails, phone messages are sometimes the result of *damage*; when severe, the result of *damage* is the pain of intimacy, and at its most perverse it is violence and violation towards others.

It's *damage* that can fuel a certain work ethic that avoids being still because to rest is to become quiet, and to become quiet is to hear the self-doubt and feel old pain. *Damage* helps us skirt commitment and wanting to say—yes! *Damage* keeps us in the war zones, and on the edge. *Damage* comes to define what it is to feel alive, and *damage* causes death by suicide.

It's often a matter of survival to wall off those feelings of damage. Yet, the friction of day-to-day life eventually makes it apparent that the calculated damage lies just beneath the surface, where we try to dig a trench and bury it. Movement, busyness, various forms of intoxication and adrenaline help push that damage wishfully below the mantle, but we all know what happens when the pressure accumulates. Little earthquakes and tremblers wake the memories, shake them loose and let the world know, something has happened here—before.

I used to get nervous whenever someone slammed a door, or if I detected, through thin walls, the sound of footsteps padding down a hallway. It wasn't real fear as much as unease. A long-standing anxiety born from my parents' berating me daily about routine things like—forcing me to take 3-minute showers; staring me down to finish everything on my plate even if it took an hour and a half to wash down buccal wads of bitter squash and mustard greens with peanut butter; repeatedly correcting my (perceived) poor penmanship; complaining whenever I left any hair in the brush which I would have to clean again. I couldn't tolerate hearing one more time about my violin practice, how imperfect it sounded, how others practiced eight hours happily compared to the measly two that I could barely stand; an ancient dread that my mother would belittle me again about how I lacked exactness, caution, and femininity. It was more the worry of an unexpected intrusion, that I'd be showered by a memory I couldn't towel off, like the sensation of my mother's fingernail pinching my earlobe as she tugged it to get my attention, letting me know I miscalculated yet another math problem; I remember her knuckles wrapping against my temples, then digging into them as she pushed my entire head away in disgust because I was incapable of accuracy. I remember the vertex of the blade of a cold meat cleaver against my chin, as my father reminded me, once again, that he had given me life and could easily take it away.

It's commonly spoken now that the body never "forgets" anything, even if memory fails us. Memory is encoded in the calf muscles that can't seem to run fast enough through the dense fog of a dimly lit nightmare; you know, those dreams where your legs don't move, no matter how fast you run. Memory is replaced by the default irrational expectation that you'll get fired for any mistake, large or small. Memory encodes distaste for even friendly feedback. Distrust comes naturally, even if you can't remember why.

And then the small injuries repeat themselves and join the collection of incidents that remind you it's not a safe world.

A landlord once invited himself into my New York City West Village studio apartment while I was asleep in the loft bed that stood five feet from the unit entrance. I bolted upright and shouted, "What the fuck?!" He slammed the door shut in an instant, without re-locking the dead bolt, saying a loud "so sorry!" as the sound of his heavy work boots thundered down the staircase of the old rent-controlled historic tenement building, as his stale body odor lingered in the air. My fist was ready, and my heart beat like it beat when I was a child.

Recently, the courts reopened since the COVID pandemic, and I was called in for jury duty. The judge introduced the players, the court clerk, the bailiff, the State's prosecutor, and the defendant, who turned around to address us potential jurors, pulling down his mask below his chin so we could appreciate his countenance. "The defendant will remove his mask so you can see him," said the judge as he described the particulars of the case. We learned that the defendant had forced oral copulation on multiple children under the age of 10. I began hyperventilating into my mask. That ancient panic rose in me, again.

The memory of an ivory faced, blue-eyed, buck-toothed copper-haired bully, pulling my hair and body towards him, rushed in, unbidden. He was my babysitter's adult son. I was often locked in a room with him, this developmentally delayed man who terrorized me as a child. Sitting in that courtroom, I scanned for all the exits.

That's *Damage*.

M Y PARENTS were damaged a different way living through Taiwanese civil unrest and the aftermath of 1947's "228." February 28 was the day after law enforcement harassed and beat a cigarette peddler one too many times (sadly, it seems every era has its Eric Gardner), triggering protests that unleashed a massacre.

What eventually followed was martial law in 1949 and decades of oppression in Taiwan. My father tells of seeing bullets riddle the foyer roof of his family house and of watching high school friends brutally executed in the rice fields. Fearing that Mao and the Communists were only a strait away from invading, one also feared being called a Communist sympathizer. Whether true or not, this often resulted in some punishment, imprisonment, or death. Generations of Taiwanese had already lived in a country under Japanese occupation, only to be followed, after "228," by a 38-year long period of authoritarianism known as the "White Terror."

My mother, who also lived through this period of authoritarianism, and who is ten years younger than my father, and the third child of eight, told me her life was *normal*. Living with little to no luxuries despite growing up as a doctor's daughter, she slept on small mats on the bare floor with her siblings. *Normal* for my mother was having a father who gambled his way through a medical practice, sometimes refusing to see patients in favor of playing Mahjong. *Normal* according to my mother back in the early 1970's in-

cluded her warnings that the letters I wrote my maternal grandmother might be opened or lost, that we had to practice caution with what books and magazines we mailed to relatives back home. Apples, especially Red Delicious, were rare in Taiwan and a precious gift you would sneak through customs. This Taiwan is difficult to imagine against the one we know today with its wealth, modernity, and universal healthcare.

What made my parents rather insensitive and sometimes cruel? My father was prone to rage. My mother preferred silent scorn; she was unsympathetic to childish tantrums. On my 12th Christmas morning, she decided I wouldn't get presents because I hadn't done the homework she'd assigned that day, and there were no amount of tears or apologies that could soften her resolve. She took the presents already wrapped and threw them away. Could I blame my parents' abusiveness on the climate of universal corporal punishment in which *they* were raised? As much as Taiwan's civil unrest must have caused some *damage* to them, I do not believe that could explain why they could not show affection, nor would a birth order theory explain their methods. My father was also the third of eight.

I think part of the misplaced anger my father had was the metaphorical castration experience of immigration; his masculinity and sense of worth was stripped from him. None of the homeland connections mattered in a place like New York City, where my family first came in 1968, to the iconic melting pot of a city that easily rendered anyone anonymous upon arrival. New Yorkers blended in with the cacophony of sirens and taxicab horns, and as *nobodies* without their social circles, my parents were building new identities while learning a new language; they were introverted and inexperienced, emotionally absent, and incredibly bothered—always. They did not understand the harms of shaming me, and they did not know how to control doing it. Driven by frustration and anger and the belief that children should have a clear sense of right and wrong and self-control, they perceived certain age-appropriate behaviors as misbehaviors or willful opposition that needed to be punished; precociousness was not shaped and nurtured. It was abhorred and beaten out.

TODAY, MY MOTHER'S appearance and industriousness belie her octogenarian status; with dyed black hair and the stylish bob she cut with the help of my father, with her quick and sure footing, along with a packed social schedule despite COVID—80 is her new 50. Through decades of assimilation challenges, her mettle and stoicism remain immutable, and with that, the source of her damage is still veiled and unclear to me. I used to yearn for her touch, some warmth, any tenderness, and although now she and I enjoy each other's company, she has yet to possess my deeper affections. At 13, she read my *secret diary* and discovered I had tried smoking tobacco. After upending my bedroom and tearing up my cherished portfolio of artwork, she told me, in a low seething voice, *Wǒ bùshì nǐ māmā. Bùyào jiào wǒ nǐ māmā. Yǒngyuǎn bùyào jiào wǒ nǐ māmā.* "I'm not your mother. Do not call me your mother. Never call me your mother again." She would remind me of that imperative in my adolescent years to follow. And whether she meant it or not, I must have taken some of that to heart.

NOW AT 90, my father's hair is snowy white, his gait is tentative and hunched, every rib is defined, and his blue-gray cataracts peer at me with mischief and innocence. Where is that man who instilled such fear in me? He has been replaced by a forgetful yet childish contrarian of a man, who is also surprisingly reflective. Now that there is time to remember, he shares memories of the days before he was damaged.

He loves recounting the same story of being a shirtless 18-year-old riding with friends in an abandoned army jeep not long before contracting tuberculosis and becoming bedridden for two years at home. He tells me in Mandarin, "I was very lucky, they just invented streptomycin, if that didn't happen, I would be dead." He says he remembers the wind. The wind, on his face and bare chest, the whoops of his classmates, the rush they all felt as they clung onto the roll bars of the open jeep during the bumpy rides down dirt paths.

I ride along with him, through this borrowed memory, imagining when my father felt free, before marriage and children, before the odd jobs and cultural humiliation; before the *astonishment* of coming to a new land, before the *shadow forces* of racism that told us *"Chinks go home!"*, before the storms of financial hardship which he weathered and reversed, and before he met me, his defiant, shameless daughter who grew up refusing to obey.

Jake Goldsmith

Disabled Thoughts

I ONLY EVER make long posts to my friends on social media that aren't just silly pictures when I'm unhappy and in a bad place. Every time I am (yet again) in hospital I am depressed, but I am safer (I think) in my hospital room.

I am in hospital this time (January 2022) partly because it is unsafe to be outside or even at home. My family have to work, my mum works in a school and schools are a primary vector for transmitting disease. Many healthcare workers are likely to be infected at home once close to their children.

My sister works in hospitality, catering to callous and uncaring people behaving recklessly as they eat and drink and party.

One of the hardest things about the pandemic as a disabled person has been watching people I know and care about do reckless shit that more or less communicates that they don't really care what my quality of life is.

My family try to keep me safe, but they can't control the actions of the wider public who may still infect them, as if it is somehow their choice to infect someone with a preventable, deadly disease. It is not one's free choice to murder others.

And then the news of what the U.K. wishes to do in March is truly murderous, without pretence. Serial killers are condemned for directly murdering people, but implementing policies that kill thousands somehow doesn't receive equal reproach. 12 years of austerity and the slow neglect and killing of disabled people was bad, this casual eugenics just continues.

It's really exhausting how many people are currently of the mind that: "I'm not a eugenicist, how dare you call me that, but also I do believe my convenience is more important than our col-lective safety and the weak and inconvenient should simply vanish from society." The pandemic being over means actually doing things to mitigate the spread of the virus and protect people from infection and death. So many believe in lies (about virology or life generally) at the expense of those most at risk. Other nations are better at this. Not doing stuff, not making sacrifices because you are weak-willed and privileged, means it will continue. Unrestricted behaviour without limitations means more death and an unfree, further inaccessible society.

Most do not care about those who haven't been able to go out and live due to the risk increased with their disability, or those who still have to but aren't given proper accommodations and support. The gall of some to say we have been successful in saving lives is a gross lie; the U.K. especially has done abysmally through this whole period.

People's words and petty defences mean less than their actions, which have only perpetuated harm towards people they revile or just do not care about.

Many disabled people and those who would still effectively be shielding are abandoned as the rest of society prefers the nasty, brutish, and short life to actually having our short time be worth anything.

I am already close to death and don't wish to be closer due to the callousness of others. Even before the pandemic my life was isolated and lonely, mostly depressed and ruminating on my shortcomings and my impending death. What's my projection? I've long maintained that it will be miraculous for me to reach 30 years old. I nearly died in May (2021). Any attempt I have to be happier or more optimistic feels like lying to myself. And each day I feel like I have less and less of an opportunity to do things. What could be considered worse in various ways than being *ex-*

plicit, obvious Nazis is that essentially millions of people across the world view mandates and their "personal freedoms" (when they are already free to do whatever the Hell they want, with no real idea of what lacking freedom actually means) as more important than life and death for vulnerable people. Do I have to temper my condemnation? Spurious ideas about "the economy" or one's own convenience and choice to be harmful matter more than death, for them. They may recoil at the most obvious fascist tendencies or violent actions yet they are fine to actively contribute to or ignore death, suffering, and the real lack of freedoms. Mass death via neglect, incompetence, and indifference to life is as savage as death by malice and intent. Statistically it amounts to the same weight in corpses. The former is less expensive too, so people can remain comfortable while it happens and convince themselves that they are actually on the side of liberty and justice while depriving us of those very things—at least the so-called explicit Nazis or eugenicists are honest and you know where they stand. At least stab me in the front.

Am I too radical? Am I too hyperbolic? Am I exaggerating? Is it all too much? I know I am so wonderfully morally superior but am I upsetting them? I'm not even a terrorist or a killer and I don't implement or support polices that kill thousands of the most vulnerable people alive, but I guess I'm the bad one.

Disability and illness, and what they represent in all their variances, have an existential weight attached to them. They are then often deliberately overlooked, undervalued, with their representations preferred dead or out of the way. One of the most fundamental aspects of existence is viewed instead as a narrow lens, a niche, rendered as unimportant or as malignant—out of fear, shame, utilitarian malevolence or stock ignorance. Misunderstood and put at a distance. Disability and its implications are reviled as they're not a comfortable presence for many people.

Popular culture in any nation will not contend with pain, grief, illness, or disability (not always synonymous, but still) in any truly commendable or genuine way. We simply do not cope with life. Disability or ill-health is viewed as a personal failure to not work or do better before it is comprehended simply as reality often inescapable reality. And the needs of disabled people will always come after the needs of those who aren't so when it most matters. Casual eugenics is the preferred state of affairs for many of us before accepting disabled life. Whole industries, much of civilisation, even, is dependent on making illness an easily comprehensible personal fault and truly escapable through enough effort, money, or spirit. Values held so commonly deem life worthless if it cannot be 'productive' in what is ultimately a terrible way to spend our short time.

Heaven forbid you make the *healthies* uncomfortable. One better not present a less than heroic image, lacking any glitzy optimism, no hard grit, or show anything that may make them a little upset. If illness is not presented in a way that makes those who aren't ill or disabled comfortable, in their aloof world removed from real concerns, then good luck. Allow me to be a bit miserable. Or if I am somehow jovial, I don't need false hope.

Pain and its minimisation, being able to be merely comfortable with the tiniest reprieve, is more important to me than most else. I am too ambivalent towards continuing life if doing so means being in an amount of pain than makes prolonging not worth the cost. This doesn't then mean drugging me into complete catatonia so I feel nothing, I simply want to live without being so exhausted, without so much stress, before my premature death that I absolutely terrified of. I don't want to shorten my life, but I end up being complacent and unable to do things that would prolong it because they cause far too much discomfort and distress.

The callous then suggest that not being able to stoically handle such pain is weakness or a moral failing. I will reserve using the worst words that I have for them.

I repeat that these people live in an entirely different and dismissive universe unattended to some of the most vital rudiments of the human condition—which involve sickness and disability. They believe the conceit that rendering life through the lens of disability is reductive, rather than experiencing life with a more essential primary theme. Obviously this does not mean that sick or disabled people are now soothsayers or immediately more knowing of the truth, and I hold no room at all for fetishisation or self-flagellating glorification, but, rather . . .

". . . this matter of ill-health is more personal, more essentially of the ego than anything in the world; more than love, for that can be given expression; more than religion, because that is a satisfaction in itself; more than fear, for that passes. Pain is personal, before everything. Only one who has experienced it in some measure can understand its significance in life." Richmond H. Hellyar in *W.N.P. Barbellion* (1926).

I just want some respite, even if true peace is impossible. Just treat people a little better.

Iván Argüelles

Inspired by Verlaine

bird in flight my little book of memories
lost and lorn the seas below and vast the blanks
between unwritten words a melancholy that
does not abate a summer session in fields
long cemented over a thrill when rhapsody
of bees in literary swarm comes into sight
longing that lasts forever for the unknown
hospice for the broken-hearted who cannot
read the invisible verses of my little book
cupola of clouds and shelter from the rains
paragraphs of little use and fragments like
rocks jutting from the shore and waters as
violent as passions can endure the sequences
of life the ways littered with loss and yearning
come what may the end is sure no nestled
comfort only grief the unstitched syllables
that punctuate the untitled poems of this
small book of verse this unpublished tome
that wings its way unconsciously soaring
blindly into the sun's blazing homophone as
if to acquire some taste of fame and oblivion
in the endless burning of its memories

04-24-22

Bradley David

Girl With A Pearl Herring

M Y MOTHER is the kind of sun-puckered asshole who brags to the women at work about the necklace her daughter made her, only to go home to that very daughter without bringing her Cheetos or Tang. Then, in the absence of my orange foods, has the nerve to bitch about those work women, somehow expecting me to care. You'd like her, though. She'd laugh at precisely the right moment you say something stupid to make her like you. But you'd get to go home after that chortling duet and I'd still have to sit by her on the sofa while she peels off her toenails.

Sometimes she gets so caught up in *American Idol* she accidentally harvests the pulp of her nailbed and then yowls like the worst contestant. But she doesn't let that stop her. She sucks air between her teeth and doubles down until the job's done. By then everything's bleeding. After a night of picking, she'll be sore and mad at herself the next morning. She'll rub coconut oil on her toes before work so they'll glide freely against each other. But she uses so much oil it soaks through the cheap leather of her high heels and makes the tips like she's stepped in a puddle of wax. Nobody dares ask her what's up with those shoes. Everybody's super sweet to my mom because she's a court clerk and she can take care of your speeding ticket with a few plasticky clicks of her fishing pole acrylics.

My toenails are painted orange. Same color as my All Stars and Orange Crush. They kind of smell like Velveeta, which I kinda like. I'm only telling you that to get the worst out of the way. I could have lied and said I don't sniff my peelings, but I try not to lie much. When I do, I eventually tell you about it.

So, I better tell you about mother's sofa. It's the same color blue as a Bic ballpoint. I know because I can write my name on the upholstery without anybody noticing. It has white cranes dancing on twisty black branches with red blossoms on the tips. Once I was rolling my head back and forth on the cushion to create static in my hair and my gum fell out. I rolled over the gob over and over and mashed it right into the fabric. And my hair. I picked and picked but it never did all come off the cushion. Eventually the pink turned black. And eventually the black turned shiny. Now it blends in pretty well with the trees. But I have to tell you, if I really give the edge a good picking, there's still some pink under there.

I lied and told my mother it was her friend Nancy's gum. Nancy is always chewing gum with her mouth open, and she talks so damn much she forgets it's in there. By some miracle it stays on course, agitating around and around like a front-load washer. Sometimes you'll see it catch her by surprise when it attempts an escape and then it gets a real smackdown. Her jaws go into overdrive, teaching it a lesson in disobedience. Once her appeased jowls regain their composure, she'll blow a few petite bubbles. Her tongue just barely sticks out of her wrinkled lip gasket to form a polite little pink pouch. Quite the feat coming from a yap like that.

Anyway, I'm just saying it's no shocker that Nancy's gum fell out onto the sofa. I mean, it didn't really, but I wouldn't have been surprised if it did. So, I told my mother that it was Nancy's ass that steam-pressed her gum into the cushion. I probably said "bum" so my mother wouldn't squirt orange Dial in my mouth. Anyway, I told you I eventually come clean about my lies and eventually I'll come clean about this one. Just as soon as I get out of here.

My dad used to call my mom's friends the Birk-N-Bags because they sit around the pool acting all fancy, collecting carcinoma and drinking cosmos like they're *Sex and the City*. Sex left that city a long time ago, my dad used to say. He'd look at them out the window and apologize that I could use a better role model. Half the time I swear he was out looking for one. I use past tense when I talk about him because he's dead.

My dad idolized me because I make pearls. I mean, my body makes them, it's not like I'm a jeweler or something. One time he stepped on a pink pearl at the bottom of our pool and he thought it must have fled the neck of one of the Birk-Ns. But it was from me. I didn't know it at the time, of course. I hocked a loogie and spit it in the pool because I was all plugged up and also wanted to see if the current was strong enough to pull it into the filter drain. But my phlegm oyster sank right to the bottom. Since I didn't know how to swim under water yet there was nothing I could do.

The origin of the pearl remained a mystery until I did it again. Only took a few months to produce another one, which is much faster than an oyster. They take five years. It stands to reason that I know more about pearls than most people. For example, I know that mine are non-nacreous which means they don't have that rainbow-like luster that oyster pearls have. Mine are more like conch pearls. Oddly shaped and sometimes pinkish but usually more of a bronchial yellow. I refuse to let my mother tell my doctor about them because I know they'll just conspire to sell me to the Bellagio. She doesn't care what I do most of the time, but she's all about me making more pearls. She has me eating three pink Tums before bed because she thinks that will make them grow faster and make them a nicer color. It's not like I'm being forced into child labor. I'd eat Tums anyway because I go through half a jar of pickled herring before bed.

Mother clings to the theory that my body makes pearls because I'm so stuck on pickled herring. Like eating it is turning me into a fish, or something. How could that even . . . *ugh*, don't get me started. I've tried to explain "science" to her a million times. Even if I did turn into a fish, I couldn't make pearls because pearls don't come from fish. Oh well, her brain swims in Triple Sec so I shouldn't expect miracles. I do love pickled

herring, though. My dad first let me taste it when I was ten. Kind of as a joke, because I always used to say, "I'll have what he's having." He thought I'd make a funny face but was surprised when I asked for more. He always ate it with chopsticks, so now I eat it with chopsticks too. He wasnt Asian, though. He was Swedish and he said that's why I have straight blonde hair like Joni Mitchell.

You know what else makes my mother a flamboyant asshole? She has brown bread and coffee for breakfast every single day because that's what Patti Smith does. She doesn't even listen to Patti; she only read about her in *Vogue*. She listens to *Train*. Anybody who listens to *Train* has no right painting her toenails black or eating brown bread. I listen to Patti. And you know what I eat when I listen to her? Whatever the fuck I feel like.

I used to care what people think. Like, I was terrified when my hair started falling out in middle school. I thought it was because I rolled around on the sofa so much, but my doctor diag nosed me with stress-induced alopecia. I had to wear a wig and I was anxious kids would be able to tell. How could they not? I mean, that thing looked like a Halloween costume. Anyway, naturally the kids found out about my wig and, man, did they ever fuck me up. It was my first year in Vegas since moving here and I learned real quick that Vegas girls are tough. A gang of three got me cornered and yanked that wig off in one tug. Where the adhesive had stuck to my scalp around the edges, my skin pulled clear off and left a constellation of bloody pinholes. I had to go to the nurse's office and that dumbass put Band-Aids on all the raw spots—stuck right onto my wispy hair. She didn't even think about the fact that I'd eventually have to pull those bandages off. That shit hurt! So, I went home and soaked a long time in the pool to loosen them up. I just floated and floated and watched leaves get sucked into the filter drain and cried and cried. That's why I hocked up that loogie and the pearl came out. I might not have their hair, but those girls can't spit pearls.

C.D. Rose

Drone/Echo

Before you read this piece, make sure the room you are in is as silent as possible. If possible, close the door, the window too. Turn off the radio, stop listening to music. Switch off any appliances that may be running. If you have noisy neighbours or barking dogs on your street, do what you can to mitigate their bother. If you are on public transport of some kind, or a café or bar, or if you are in an open air space, find the quietest angle you can, far from chatter, traffic, the sound of wind or water. Do not put ear plugs in. Do not read this piece aloud.

Listen.

At first, you may hear only silence, but very soon you will notice the throng of this silence: the hum of the fridge or gurgle of a radiator, the whirr of a computer. Stop these, if you can. The ticking of a clock will become deafening. Traffic may sigh in the distance, or you may notice the grudging rumble of a train. You will hear the silence itself, its thickness, its dust.

Try to ignore the distractions (the passing car, the purring cat) and listen harder: find what is beneath that pleasant hush (or does it disturb you already?) Identify, if you can, the sounds beneath the silence, for surely there are some, wherever you are: wind in the eaves; the 60 cycle per second whirr of step-down transformers on telephone poles; overhead wires; a neighbour's uneasy footsteps; wine glasses. Pick one of these and concentrate on it for one moment.

Now begin reading.

Echo was a mountain-dwelling nymph, an Oread from Mount Cithaeron. Once, when Hera was again trying to catch Zeus red-handed, Echo tried to distract her with chatter and babble, but Hera wanted none of it and cursed her distractor: Echo was only able to repeat the last words spoken to her.

Drone is a sound frequency ranging from 30 Hz up to 12 000 Hz, the former being a low rumble and the latter a high-pitched whistle, each scarcely audible.

Soon after, Echo fell in love with Narcissus, but could not tell him so. Narcissus, confused and irritated by the repetitive reverberation, spurned her. Echo's body wasted from sadness. Her voice was all that remained.

Rocks are Echo's bones; Echo's bones are Drones.

In another version of the story, Echo is a charm with a quicksilver voice. Pan takes a fancy but Echo spurns him, and Pan in turn whips up a frenzied horde to tear her to pieces. Gaia, filled with pity, hides the million shreds of Echo's body in the loneliest places. Even guilty Pan heard her, and, tormented, chased the sounds, never to catch as much as a whisper.

Were Drone a mythical figure, they would be a deity benthic or chthonic, one of low places and undergrounds. Like Echo, Drone would be ubiquitous and invisible. A troll or giant snake, a sea serpent or ouroboritic worm dwelling in frosty Nordic mountains, Celtic barrows, Sardinian nuraghe, or the fathomless ocean. A dragon, even, in deep subterranean slumber.

The builders of the great medieval cathedrals knew about Echo. In Chartres, Burgos, and Ely, you can hear her: maybe those masons and architects, too, had parts of her body buried in the vaults and buttresses, the domes and dark entries. In the cathedrals, plainchant became polyphony. Some believed Echoes were sprites which could be entranced and captured by the daisywheels or hexfoils they scratched into the walls of the old buildings.

Drone is the reverberation of the big bang, what remains of the birth of the universe.

Pause for a moment, and concentrate on listening again. Close your eyes if it helps. Listen to the silence, or better, the sounds within that silence. Focus on a detail, then open out to listen to the entire field of sound. Move back and forth between the specific and the general as you continue to read.

In 1608, on the run and hiding out in Sicily, Caravaggio visited an ancient cave near Syracuse. The grotto, some 25 metres high and winding back nearly a hundred into the rock, has a tall thin entryway, almost serpentine in form. Caravaggio's guide, the architect and archaeologist Vincenzo Mirabella, told him the legend of the tyrant who had used the cave as a prison, exploiting the space's acoustic properties to eavesdrop on his captives' whispered conversations (chiefly that of the poet Phyloxenus of Cythera, there imprisoned for having failed to praise the tyrant's awful poetry.) Caravaggio listened, and looked: 'It has the form of an ear,' he said, and using the name of the ancient imprisoner, called it the *Ear of Dionysius*. Perhaps, though, he wasn't thinking only of the tyrant but the almost-homonymous god Dionysus, and one of his avatars, Pan, and what Pan did to Echo.

Drone is the sound things make when you're not listening to them.

The Temple of Mercury at Baia near Naples is a home of Echo. It could have been a temple to her, had she ever been deified, but it was never really a temple anyhow, only later designated one by 18th century Romantics. Most probably, it was the frigidarium, for the post-sauna chill. Now, a very shallow pool has formed in it and a tree grows from the ceiling. The Temple is almost perfectly circular, and if you walk to the end of the small half-bridge which extends into the pool, and speak, your voice will return to you, perfectly, from several different angles. It accidentally prefigures the cupola of Brunelleschi's duomo in Florence, the whispering gallery of the Alhambra or the Gol Gumbaz in Bijapur. At Clonmacnoise Abbey in Ireland there is a whispering arch, where you can utter a name at one side for it to pass almost perfectly to the ear of someone standing at the base of its opposite. The arch was for confessions, marriage proposals, and for lepers to speak without fear of contamination.

Drone and Echo are non-identical twins.

In Chinon there is a Rue de l'Écho, and a sign directing you to the Echo which forms around the edge of the town's medieval walls. If you follow the sign, however, you still might not find her. Such is Echo's nature.

Without Drone, there is no music. Drone is the base in relation to which all other notes are perceived, an auditory and psychological mechanism. Drone is the rest on which any melody finally resolves. Drone, a basso profondo and continuo, anchors music to the earth, stopping it from disappearing into the aether. If it resonates in E flat, then it *is* the earth, rendered in sound.

In 1537 Niccolò Fontana Tartaglia published the *Nova Scientia*. Mostly known as a counter-Aristotelian study of motion, ballistics, and projectile trajectories, Book 4 of the *Scientia* concerns sound: Tartaglia puts forward the idea that Echo can be separated from its source, and used as a weapon of war.

Listen again. Somewhere, in your sound field, there is a Drone. Identify it, and as you continue to read, make sure you are aware of the sound, constantly, all along.

The human response to Drone is replicate it, using bodies, and tools.

Lazzaro Spallanzani was an Italian priest who, among other things, studied Echo. He had a pet owl who, he noted, hit the walls when it tried to fly indoors in the dark; bats, he also noted, didn't. This led Spallanzani to believe that bats had an extra sense and in 1793 he set to experimenting, at first covering bats' eyes with birdlime, then removing them completely. He found they could still locate tiny nesting holes in the roof of a cave in total darkness. He filled brass tubes with wax and turpentine and used them to block the bats' ears, then punctured their eardrums, before eventually acknowledging the ear as an organ of navigation.

Overtone singing originated in Mongolia or southeastern Siberia, and spread as far as Japan, Sardinia and the Sami singers of northern Sweden and Finland who breathe in a circular motion and alter the shape of their mouths' resonant cavities. They become Drone.

Echo lives in music: call and response chants, the round or canon, the counterpoint and the fugue are all about Echo. Orlando di Lasso's *O la o che bon echo*, written, perhaps, to be sung in a side chapel of one of those great cathedrals, is a part song all of Echo, a whimsical dialogue between a voice and its invisible double.

The hollowed trunk of a eucalyptus in Australia, the pipes and hurdy-gurdy in Europe, the tambura in India, all dating back thousands of years, all human methods of summoning Drone.

Four hundred years after Lasso, the invention of the Echoplex changed the sound of music. Allied with radio and playback technologies, voices with no sources were everywhere: Joe Meek heard a new world, Stockhausen sang of the young ones, Lee Perry built an ark, Arthur Russell fashioned a world of Echo.

Right now, I can hear a clock ticking, a washing machine, and two other sounds which I cannot identify.

Echo appears in the margins of a number of folk tale collections, from Basile to Straparola, to Perrault and the Grimms. The uncollected tale sometimes called 'The Echo-Bird' or 'Peter and the Echo,' recasts Echo as a winged creature, a premonitor of doom, a bad omen.

I can find no record of Drone in folk story, but Drone is always there.

Are you still listening?

People all over the world can hear the Hum, and the Hum is a manifestation of Drone.

The Hum has many sources: in certain places it is the mating call of the toadfish; at 30-40 Hz it is the sound of the jet stream, up to 60 Hz it is the resonant frequency of buildings responding to powerlines.

Spallanzani's work tangentially gave birth to radio and detection ranging: although radar uses electromagnetic waves of frequency and not the voice, its principles are the same. If you have lost someone, you may call out their name in an attempt to find them. This, too, is a form of echolocation.

The Hum is the Drone is low frequency radio waves, used for military purposes.

The now-disused Royal Navy Fuel Tanks at Inchindown in the Scottish Highlands are six reinforced concrete chambers, each over 200 metres long, ten metres wide with fifteen metre-high arched roofs. They were built in the Second World War, and designed to be blast proof. If you say someone's name in there, that name will resonate for 112 seconds at 125 hertz. The tanks have the longest echo of any human-built structure.

The Hum is the Drone, the sound of work: air compressors, power plants, electricity substations. The Hum is the Drone is the sound of deep sea shipping coming to shore. The Hum is the Drone is the sound of steelworks, coalmines, cooling towers, and their ghosts.

Is it still there? Has it changed? Have you become used to it? Has it shifted? Listen again. Make sure you can hear the Drone.

In 1928 Elvira Lawrence, a former motorcycle stunt rider, built the Echodrome just outside Reno, Nevada. Her great intention was to create something that would be no mere carnival sideshow, but a temple to Echo. (It is possible that it was inspired by a visit to the Temple of Mercury, or the Whispering Gallery of St Pauls in London.) A long, smooth oval white wall (not unlike a motorcyclist's Wall of Death) was recessed at regular intervals with spaces for singers or musicians. Clara Rockmore, with her then fiancé, the inventor Leon Theremin, is said to have debuted her own First Concerto there, but no recording remains. After a grisly murder case centred on the Echodrome the place became a destination for rubber-necking tourists from Reno then fell into disuse during the 1940s. Its ruins still stand there today, and visitors claim its Echo is more potent than ever.

One Hum theory claims that it consists of spontaneous otoacoustic emissions, the sound our own ears make. We are Drone.

Echolalia is the spontaneous habit of repeating the sounds other people, or things, make. It is a common process in language acquisition, and can be a symptom of various autism spectrum disorders.

Drone doesn't know what time it is, and doesn't care: Drone dissolves time.

Echo is the presence of the disembodied; Echo is a ghost.

In one of the ninety stories in *Indeterminacy*, John Cage wrote about visiting the anechoic chamber at Harvard University. 'In that silent room,' he wrote, 'I heard two sounds, one high and one low.' He asked the engineer why, if the room was so silent, he had heard two sounds. 'The high one was your nervous system in operation,' said the engineer, 'and the low one your blood in circulation.'

When you, too, are in a lonely place, Echo will be there: a haunting of wild mercury.

The Om is the first sound, the Drone almighty, the act of creation itself.

How much time has passed since you began to read? Do you know?

Where Drone and Echo meet they form a sound we recognise as running water, thundering rain, the static hiss of electronic devices, tuned-out radios, applause. It is a complex sound, capable of drowning others. It is a mighty roar and an insidious hiss.

All Drones are vibrations, all Echoes too. All sound is movement.

Drones and Echoes are not only polyphonic, but also polysemic. Now, Drone is a multirotor unmanned aerial vehicle; Echo a smart speaker housing a voice-controlled personal assistant.

If you hot desk in an open plan office, some of your colleagues will be wearing noise-cancelling headphones, or ear buds, at least. If you commute by train or bus, you will see workers with them clamped to their heads. *(Maybe you are wearing them now, as you read this.)* Many of those people are listening to white noise. They claim it helps them focus, concentrate. Drone music is 21st century worksong.

Are you still listening? Don't forget to listen.

The town of Agnone in Molise is home to the Pontificia Fonderia Marinelli, a thousand-year old bell forge. Each year, every church in the valley in which the town lies plays one note on its bells, and this note is responded to by the next church along the valley. Even with the best vantage point, a listener will never be able to hear more than five or six of the forty churches' bells ringing. The piece is all Echo, and all Drone, and can never be heard in its entirety.

And here, feel free to listen for—or imagine—an Echo, too. A high-pitched sound, pinging around your room, head or reading space, slowly ebbing, dying, fading away . . .

Drone is depression, a howl of anguish; Echo is laughter, giddy, rising. Echo is hysteria, a compacted scream; Drone is profound joy, the deep well-spring of connectedness to the earth.

Listen! Can you hear?

Jack Foley

RATTALK

It becomes clear that the "ground" of European thought is a "rift" (*Riss*). It is impossible to deepen or cancel out this "rift" into a "unity" or "identity." Nevertheless, European thought tends to affirm the stable "presence" of its essential categories. . .It would have to be the case that the notion of stable entities—and their operative conceptuality—is in fact unfounded.

—Peter Trawny, *Heidegger A Critical Introduction*

I'M HALF IRISH and half Italian. My two favorite poets are Yeats and Dante.

I lost my faith but I still have my begorrah.

Eyes. Yes.

The famous poet went on and on about how difficult it was to achieve this poem. He tried once, and it failed. Tried again; failed. Et cetera. I wondered whether he shouldn't take up another line of work.

Poetry should be a pleasure, not a task.

These sox are on their last legs.

I'm as much a *wronger* as a *writer*.

Some is well.

What if the search to discover "mind" is self-defeating because "mind" doesn't exist? What if "mind" is a term made up out of a puritanical impulse to separate thinking from the body—but has no actual existence? We say "mind thinks," but if mind doesn't exist this statement is meaningless. The statement nevertheless creates a false dualism because the moment we say "mind," we *oppose* it to "body." What if *thinking is an activity of the body*—like walking or peeing? What I'm saying doesn't imply that trying to discover mind is a fruitless endeavor. Like Columbus, you may discover all kinds of things in the effort to discover mind. It's just that—if mind is a fictional entity, nothing but a verbal construct—you won't discover mind because: *it isn't*. To put it another way: What if "mind" is only a kind of medium—the way paint is a medium? The means by which an activity can take place. We have a capacity to think as we have a capacity to walk, but we don't necessarily have "a mind" in the way that we have legs. We have a brain, yes, and it's part of our body. But not a "mind."

When I hear people say that poetry is "essentially speech," basically an oral art, I wonder about all that concrete poetry—poetry like e.e. cummings' "grasshopper," poetry that *can't be spoken*. Isn't that poetry?

I used to be 6 foot 7 before we had a child. (Before I took up poetry.)

A mango is a peach that died and went to heaven.

It is possible, even after all these years, that *Plato was wrong.*

When I wrote film criticism, I wasn't interested in telling people whether a film were good or bad: I was interested in finding out what I was doing there in the dark.

Revision is addition, not subtraction.

Picture me as a line of chorus girls. We're all tap dancing and we need to get off the stage for the next act to come on. So we're given a "traveling step." The most famous traveling step of all time is Shuffle Off to Buffalo. (Jack demonstrates, leaves the room.)

No influence. I had already settled into what I was doing. But the discovery of an almost totally unknown—and totally forgotten—master. The quality of the work was no guarantee of fame. No one has heard of him whereas (compared to him) more or less mediocre poets are in everyone's consciousness. Never a poem in *The New Yorker.* Never any students to spread the word. No other poets singing his praises. The sheer loneliness of his work is stunning. He must have thought that someone would pick up on it. Work of this quality won't simply vanish. Yet that is exactly what it did.

Timor mortis conturbat me.

(After dinner.) Why is Jack like Trigger? Because he's *stuffed.*

If you don't have any place better to go, you can always go to the bathroom.

The secret to a happy relationship is "Yes, dear." (Sangye: "Yes, dear.")

Timor mortis conturbat me.

Do tough guys in Brooklyn still say *dese* and *dose* for *these* and *those*? The Greek words for god and goddess are *theos* and *thea.* The Roman words are *deus* and *dea . . . The Romans were tough guys, too!* ("Yes, we were," says William Fasolino.)

As for individualism, the term goes back to the Latin *individuus,* which means not divided. I have no problem if the term is used in a political sense, as in the rights of the individual. But if it is used to describe what is going on in my head—psyche—then it seems to me nonsensical. I am as divided as I can be, so I am not an individual, not *individuus.* What I think I am is a multiplicity. It is the damaging propaganda of capitalism, of consumerism that persuades people that they are individuals. If people really were individuals—separate, different—then Madison Avenue would have no power over them, and it has immense power over them. Trump's followers, who believe his lies, believe themselves to be individuals. That is the true blossoming of consumerism.

These days capitalism depends to a considerable extent on finding "hidden persuaders"—subliminal elements—that convince people to buy things they neither need nor want. What happens to your "free not to buy something" in that situation? You can find these persuaders even in the realm of popular song. For a song to be "popular" it has to be remembered. Who can forget a song that begins with the command, "You must remember this"? Many other examples. Popular songs are in the realm of capitalism too. You have to "buy" them. And we measure value not in terms of life-changing experiences but in terms of sales. A million seller. Poetry, they tell us, doesn't sell. But perhaps that's an advantage. Rilke tells us that the point of art is to *change your life: Du mußt dein Leben ändern.*

Belief in choice is an assertion of good Protestant values—values which go very well with capitalism. Back in the day, if a priest and an Irishman were walking on a hill and the priest asked the name of the hill. The Irishman might well have said, "That hill is sacred to Bridget, our red-headed goddess of fire, the hearth, poetry." "Good," says the priest, "she'll be Saint Bridget now." That is precisely the kind of thing that the Protestants were protesting—the presence in Christianity of Pagan elements, elements like the Christmas tree. Against the Catholic impulse to be inclusive—to be "catholic"—the Protestants insisted on choice, on "either/or" in Kierkegaard's phrase. This is why the Protestants invented divorce—individual choice inserted into the institution of marriage—and why the great Protestant poem is *Paradise Lost,* a poem which is all about a wrong choice.

Consumerism creates a kind of metaphysics of individuality and choosing—affirming individuality (or ego) by choosing. It's not that choice doesn't exist but that it is far less extensive than it is given credit for being. It may well be that what we represent to ourselves as "choices" are nothing but the promptings of a situation which in fact determines why we move in one direction or another. Isn't that the lesson of Freud and others? What about the concept of "fate"? Perhaps "fate" is one's situation. If one ceases to believe passionately in individuality (which doesn't mean that one therefore begins to believe passionately in the opposite of individuality, "the crowd") then having to choose one thing rather than another becomes far less important. Consumerism loves choosing. Buy this rather than that. But choice may be damaging. Why not both/and rather than either/or? Why not an entirely new arrangement of possibilities? Assertions that certain things are "best" arise out of this emphasis on choosing. The "best" is "the chosen one." What if there is no "best"? What kind of poetry arises out of a consciousness opposed to individuality and choosing? Choose.

Peeeeeeeople!!

Xugioytrecxzasdkoplbwerq!

Some grease is natural, some grease is acquired.

Yoda knows all about the force but has yet to master elementary English grammar. "Stupid am I."

The most difficult thing about a poetry reading is getting out of the room afterwards.

KPFA: how do you spell that? (T-h-a-t.)

I sometimes think that if you didn't have self-pity you couldn't have popular songs.

Every modern convenience tends to isolate people in their houses. Covid-19 has accelerated this process.

The silence and whiteness of the page.

Speaking of Larry Eigner, Michael McClure said, "It's like a Martian consciousness."

Scone, like *done*; scone, like *stone*. Basil Bunting's complaints about "the barbarous American pronunciation," scone, like stone. Hutch sings *telephun*—like *done*. "A telephun that rings but who's to answer?"

There is God, there is Heaven, and there is Chai. (Not necessarily in that order.)

You wanna know how to start a religion? Find something people *really* like to do. Call it a sin. You have a religion. Tell them they will die. Tell them you can save them from death and from the horrible consequences of death. But tell them you will only save them from death if they do as you say.

"Breasts, madam."

Collage has been called, by Jerome Rothenberg and others, *the* art form of the twentieth century, and collage by its very nature moves *against* the idea of private property. Did T.S. Eliot ask permission of all the people he quoted in *The Waste Land*?

Not collage: collision!

"The disease of choosing."

Language is what you do with your *langue*. Writing is not language.

The ancient Greek seeing lightning, hearing thunder
Would have attributed it to Zeus
We know that Zeus Pater never existed except in a communal imagination
So the attribution is wrong

But the thunder and lightning were real
The thunder and lightning were real

(Angry) These writers are in paper bags. Some of the paper bags are more substantial than others, but they're all in paper bags. Not one of them has a new idea about the art. Not one of them can write his way out of a paper bag.

A thought about voices and characters: Both Pound and Eliot were reading Browning. Browning creates various voices, but it is always one voice per poem. Both Pound and Eliot get the idea of writing a single poem in which there are various voices rather than only one. This creates disturbing issues about selfhood and the notion of "unity" for both of them. Eliot actually claims in a note that *The Waste Land* is, like Browning's work, a dramatic monologue, that the entire poem is spoken by Tiresias. This is possible, says Eliot, because Tiresias is both male and female, so he can be all the voices of the poem. But this "explanation" falls to pieces when you realize that Tiresias is not both young and old and there are young and old voices in Eliot's poem. Worse, Eliot also believes that his discovery of multiple voices means that he is a playwright. His plays are demonstrations that this is not the case! He is not creating a poem of various "characters" as a playwright creates various characters in a play. The interplay of voices in *The Waste Land* is not the interplay of characters. Eliot is responding to—creating an "objective correlative," an equivalent to—the various voices and contexts constantly present in his mind.

Denunciations of our society are easy enough to make—there is a lot in our society that requires denouncing—but, unless the denouncer cops to some sort of complicity, the denunciations carry with them a strong egoistic element. The real subject of such screeds is not the society they are supposedly denouncing but the self-satisfaction one feels at being totally in the right. The "text" is the horrors of society—which everyone knows about—but the "subtext" is the ego gratification of the speaker. Denunciatory poems are popular for that reason. The audience experiences the pleasure of hearing something they already agree with—so their complacency isn't challenged. Such poems change absolutely nothing and don't urge anyone to *do* anything: their perpetrators would be horrified to know that they are really an assertion of the status quo.

The essays in the *N.Y. Review of Books* are all about the satisfaction of being *done* with a subject: Thank God that's settled; I don't have to think about *that* anymore.

His brow was never furrowed by the plow of Thought.

Latin as magic: the word *spell*, meaning to list the letters of a word, is the same as *spell* used in casting a spell. To have access to reading was to have the power of magic. Every book a grimoire. It's said that "hocus pocus" derived from *Hoc est corpus meum*. Derived/*river*.

Sometimes I don't need to go someplace. I can just send this shirt. (I can just send this hat.)

My writing is extremely varied but the task is not to unify these variations. The task is to find a structure which can contain them all. *The task is not to lose any.*

Yeats' "Turning and turning in the widening gyre, / The falcon cannot hear the falconer" is not what it is usually interpreted to be: an image of chaos. It's an image of *escape*. The falconer is trying to bring the bird/soul down to the earth, where everything is a horror. It's the only moment in the poem where Yeats suggests *another way*, an alternative to the way of the beast.

God creates *ex nihilo*, out of nothing: there is no "world" until God "creates" it. The poet's "creativity" is not like that. The poet *inhabits* a world which is always impinging upon him/her. The poet "creates" *from that world*, not from nothing. For this reason, the poet's "creativity" is significantly different from God's; it is closer to that of the jazz musician who is always reacting to something given: a set of chords, a tune. But this notion of Goddish "creativity" has a secret consolation, a secret pleasure: it expresses the desire to *forget* what I have just said, to imagine oneself as God-like—without precedent, without history. "Poet, be like God," wrote Jack Spicer.

The primary insight of the now defunct, not wholly unlamented twentieth century is the perception that *some parts of the mind don't know what other parts of the mind are doing.*

What kind of poetry emerges out of a notion of the mind as multiple, as simultaneously open and closed to itself?

It's not that great to turn 70, but you get a good word: *Septuagenarian. Octogenarian*—if you make it to that—is good too.

The myth of the Individual, of personal, singular experience seems to be finally dying, thank the Loud, though it is an extremely slow, complex dying. What new myths, what new forms of expression are possible for us? (Do new myths, new forms of expression necessarily involve violence?)

No man is an I. (No woman either.)

Speaking of his film, *Natural Born Killers*, the movie director, Oliver Stone said, "Violence! I'm against violence! But did you expect me to make a dull movie?"

She stood before me with a smoking gun, looking down at her husband's dead body. "I didn't do it," she said. I believed her.

What happens is not that there is the book and there is ourselves as individuals and they are in a relationship: what happens is that *we enter the field of language*. Language generates a world in which it is the primary event—in which it postulates reality. The power of rhetoric is that it creates an area which depends upon its own contexts, its own connections. Though we may respond to a book about fathers with thoughts about our own father or a book about mothers with thoughts about our mother, that is not the primary thing that is happening to us. What is happening is that we are being pulled into a world that is deeply and essentially NOT this world—and we enter into it happily in order to *escape* what is precisely our "individuality." All rhetoric is fiction: all reading is empathy and escape.

I enjoy *writing between the lines*—lines other people have written.

JESUS AS HENNY YOUNGMAN:

Take me. Please.

. . .

I tell ya He was the first Jew to do stand-up. "Behold thy mother." Yuck yuck yuck.

MRS. NUSSBAUM WRITES A BOOK

"Ah, Mrs. Nussbaum, I understand you have written a new book." "Have I written a new book, Mr. Allen, I have written a new tome. My husband Pierre says he should put it next to the door to stop the door." "A doorstopper, eh, Mrs. Nussbaum." "You shouldn't drop it on your foot, Mr. Allen." "Is it next to the bed for bedside reading?" "This book is not only next to the bed, it almost is the bed. Pierre put a blanket on it and got in. He finally got to sleep at Chapter Six." "Well, we'll be looking for it in the book stores, Mrs. Nussbaum." "They are giving away with it a free blanket. Arrive-a-derchi, Mr. Allen."

. . . gratitude to Gershwin for that moment
of utter magic,
guiding me, a child,
with his consummate mastery
into the deepening
dark.

THE LIVING AIR: FOR SUSAN LANDAUER (1958–2020)

no life, no matter how long
is complete.
the chaos we defy
daily
has to win in the end.
no thought, no matter how deep
is ever finished.
you loved art
and spoke of it
with great eloquence.
you loved laughter
and sought it out.
no one can say
you failed to make a difference.
no one can say
your life was
without meaning.
the words I recorded
in 1996
echo in my mind
and will echo
until my own passing
and perhaps beyond.
no mind
as good as yours,
no thought as deep
ever vanishes entirely.
you touched those
who may not even know
they were touched by you.
the ocean
gathers all its entities
living and dead
and moves deliberately on
into the living
air.

FOR JOHN M. BENNETT (1942–)

I sailed
On the sloop
John B
Ooooooo
We capsized
Baby
And lOOk
What we found:
All the fishes
All the fissures
Of
The
Deep
Blue
Sea.

oh,
another poet who thinks
Yeats couldn't tell
a great-rooted blossomer

from a tree.
Yeats lasts
but at the expense
of people understanding

his work.
Immortality is yours,
dear poet,

but no one
will know
the strangeness of your heart

Haibun de la Serna: 99 Neo-Barroco Haibun
Paul Nelson
Goldfish Press, 2022

Your goal is beyond poetry
From Haibun #47

PAUL NELSON is a once in a generation poet in the organic tradition of Charles Olson, Denise Levertov and Michael McClure. The author of *American Sentences* and *A Time Before Slaughter*, Nelson has struck again. This time, in *Haibun de la Serna*, he reimagines the ancestral Japanese genre of the *Haibun* (prose poem + haiku) as a contracting and expanding universe of neo-baroque, surreal, and abstract gestures. Added to this unique subversion, each one of the 99 *Haibun* in the collection, is inspired by a *greguería*, those witty, poetic one-liners created by Spanish avant-garde poet Ramón Gómez de la Serna such as the one that goes *Rivers do not know their names* or *A carbon copy is taken of everything that is said in the dark.*

These *greguerías* function as a gateway to a world of expressive possibilities, a stream of energy and consciousness into which Nelson dives soul first, mindfully and mindlessly. Like Terence, nothing is alien to Nelson. Nothing is irrelevant: the intimate memory and the geopolitical disquisition, runic alphabet, kim chi pierogies, Federico García Lorca, Dick Cheney, phytoplankton, Quiznos tunamelts, pepsi, tsampa, Molotov cocktails, Mickey Mouse, Abu Ghraib, dental records, eggs or Amtrak. This chaotic accumulation is not, however, poetic reflection of a random, fragmented world. *Haibun de la Serna* emerges rather as another *Aleph*, the *multum in parvo*, the miraculous, limitless, dizzying point in space that contains all other points. And as it happens in the story by Jorge Luis Borges, these *Haibun*, just like the original *Aleph*, allow us to see *in a single gigantic instant millions of acts both delightful and awful.*

Yet, that *unimaginable universe* contained in the vibrancy of a dense poetic form, winds up bursting through the seams of grammar, giving us the experience of a language flickering at the edge of meaning, and of meaning breaking to the point of collapse. These poems, like all great poems, open up towards the unnamable. Nelson's poetry is what remains after the shock wave, the pulsing blast of a genuine and audacious assault on meaning. As if following Donna Haraway's dictum that "grammar is politics by other means", Nelson ventures away from the matrix of language and its underlying logic of hegemonic power allowing us to glimpse "*a non-conceptual or prereflective mode of consciousness*" (83).

If there is a certain exhilarating *pathos* permeating this collection; there is also, underneath it, an overwhelming feeling of discontent. Discontent towards evil, towards *"the enemy we keep feeding" (the cruel majority, the dark Satanic mills,* as William Blake would call it), a weary recognition that we are all wandering like zombies in this no man's land that extends between late capitalism and our impending demise. If writing poetry appears in Nelson as the ultimate form of activism, it is not an activism narrowly conceived as political, but rather an activism in its broadest metaphysical sense.

In *The Open: Man and Animal*, Giorgio Agamben writes: "(. . .) determining the border between human and animal [is] not just one question among many discussed by philosophers and theologians, scientists and politicians, but rather a fundamental metaphysico-political operation in which alone something like 'man' can be decided upon and produced." (21) It is in this vein that Nelson speaks of "the animal self we left behind for hamburgers, traffic cameras and cappuccino" (12). Indeed, these collection of *Haibun* which also presents itself as a bestiary (mythical stags and goats, squirrels, crabs, urchins, snakes, bears, orcas, sea lions, deer, coyote, racoons, cats, ants, slugs, whales, woodfrogs, and so on) offers a poetic roadmap towards that threshold where, as Agamben would say, *Paradise calls Eden back into question*. In fact, Nelson's own *poetics* is articulated in terms that foregrounds this metaphysico-political separation between humanity and animality: "The poem less a recipe and more the salient of Crick's edgeless biology & the light therefore shot off from" (19).

This 21st century Howl, this post-historical growl, this visceral scream of a voice being torn apart is consistently probing the boundaries beyond which we are forced to confront the animal we left behind, probing in the same gesture the limits of language and of poetry:

> Scorn stays west of the left ventricle the poet says & sees it stuck there unable to mutter anything but GRAHHR or muuurrrrrffffffffff so

writes a poem that becomes a series of poems that becomes a house & a whole slum of them headed for the same plight (evening) stuck in the shithole of his imagination up near the top of the monkey puzzle tree to wile away the January afternoon hoping not to become lunch for Sasquatch/lost in the dust of a library archive waiting to return in another incarnation or vivid hallucination. (Haibun # 54, p. 57)

Hence, *Haibun de la Serna* could be read as an attempt to get unstuck and move beyond language, beyond humanity, beyond poetry. In its Zen-like impulse this book is also about going beyond by staying in place; surrendering as a method of attack. That's one way of understanding the sentence by Zen master Dōgen that opens the collection: "When you find your place where you are, practice occurs." Paul Nelson's poetry is this place of immanence and transcendence at the same time. We still don't know what lays beyond poetry. We are all stuck in the monkey puzzle. We do have the feeling, however, after reading *Haibun de la Serna* that we are also somehow closer to "practice", yearning for a space beyond ourselves. . .

Small Moods
Shane Kowalski
Future Tense Books, Portland, Oregon, 2022

T HE GROWING PLACE of flash fiction is everywhere evident and Shane Kowalski's *Small Moods* demonstrates the ready appeal of the form. Here, intriguing storytelling nuggets resist the conventions of literary realism which all too often seems less a window onto the world than an incomplete or even lazy cop-out to avoid the strangeness and intensity of human experience.

No shortage of strangeness here. A story called "Cats Cannot Kill Themselves" begins, "I was looking for a job and found one as a house cat." How could I not read on? In another story, "Deathwatch" the narrator decides to throw clocks into a cooking pot, explaining, "It matters that we don't know! I love that we can't see!"

Kowalski, to his credit, seems allergic to manifestos or didacticism—but the above statement nonetheless describes an overall sensibility or aesthetic for this collection: a contrarian refusal of authorial pretensions of knowing and seeing.

In "The Black Jeweled Box of Clarity," we are told that "we can open the black jeweled box of clarity, but we can't understand how to use what's in it." In "Inheritance," the narrator announces, "I am like the candle that gives out darkness." The best pieces of *Small Moods* artfully dramatize how any hope of clarity about human predicaments must necessarily allow for the arbitrary, the inscrutable and obscure.

Most of these stories are very short, only a page or two—this seems to be Kowalski's preferred form. Some pieces, to my taste, seem prompt-like with a flavor of a notebook entry, and they leave me wishing the writer had followed through at *a little* more length, not to naturalize or explain their peculiarity but rather to amplify their originality and do them justice.

Some of the best pieces embrace the fairy tale form, and serve as a reminder that flash fiction and it violent ambiguities have deep roots. "The Magic Orgasm" begins

> A peasant boy, leading his family's dairy cow back from grazing, came across a troll who offered him a trade. For your cow, dear boy, I will offer you an orgasm, said the troll.
>
> The peasant boy looked at the troll. That doesn't seem like a fair trade, said the peasant boy.
>
> Ah! said the troll. This is no ordinary orgasm though. This is a magic orgasm! Here, see for yourself!
>
> The troll held it out in his hand, the size of a bean, green and glowing.

A logic is set in motion, full of consequences against a backdrop of darkness. Or, in a delightful story called "The Gerbil Finds You"

> Sixty-three years later, the lost gerbil finds you again on the sidewalk. It has rheumatism and walks with a cane now.
>
> You adjust your bifocals on your nose to see clearer this vision from your youth.
>
> Herbert! My god, I've missed you, you say when you recognize him.
>
> Yes, yes, Herbert says.
>
> We all thought you died, you say. One day you were just gone and we thought you died.
>
> Yes, yes, Herbert says. I did not.

Herbert's ensuing testimony is crushing, and marks the first time that this reviewer has been crushed by a gerbil. Other strong pieces include "These Kind of Things" and the closing story, "The Hand Dances" which, incidentally, are the longest pieces in *Small Moods* and might not qualify as flash fiction at all.

All told, this is original work, uncompromising and sometimes harsh, yet vulnerable and engaging.

Beyond Repair
J.C. Todd
Able Muse Press, San Jose, California, 2021

THIS LATEST poetry collection by J.C. Todd addresses the price of war from a multitude of perspectives and though—unfortunately—it is timely, it is also impressive for its range across continents and cultures. Todd is at pains to look beyond framed narratives that, consciously or not, we bring to this human-made catastrophe. As the poem "Cover Shot" reminds us, our imaginations yearn for glossy images, "the cropped shot" or "a good story" even as "the background resists / insists."

Beyond Repair explores that resisting, insisting background. Reading this book, I was reminded of Philip Larkin's observation that "at the bottom of all art lies the impulse to preserve." Although in many ways different from Larkin (implied temperament and politics, for starters), Todd is tenacious about preserving. What gets cropped out of many accounts can in fact be crucial with respect to the larger picture.

The collection begins with "In Whom the Dying Does Not End," about the destruction of Hama, Syria, by Hafez al-Assad, an atrocity which to this day remains a local taboo about which one does not speak. The poem's speaker contemplates her pregnancy during this time and her daughter's arrival into this world of "playing fields and killing / floors." Mothers and daughters, who are prime examples of figures who are often cropped out of accounts of war, are central to this book, in contexts as various as the Arab Spring and the American War in Iraq to the ghetto of Pylimo Gatvé in Vilnius or the situation of a World War II Japanese "War Bride."

In the poem "The heart doesn't have four chambers yet," a mother goes out amid rubble

"into the scorched-walled garden
to dig up unsinged bulbs she'll chop like shallots
and simmer behind the blackout drapes,
a bitter broth, all there is to feed the unborn one."

"FUBAR'd" is a longer poem sequence that recounts the experiences of a woman working as a military doctor in the American War in Iraq. One harrowing anecdote concerns a grievously-wounded soldier and the doctor's heroic efforts to evacuate him which leave her feeling, nonetheless, disgusted: she is "packaging a lie" because the evacuation represents a politically-motivated attempt to lower the war-zone body count. Even the most vulnerable are instrumentalized, so "this mercy flight's a take-out / delivery."

Many of the poems are written in free verse, using speech rhythm and sometimes surprising enjambments, though "FUBAR'd" uses sonnet convention, "Gates" is a diptych, and there are also prose poems. Most poems depend on a detailed specificity but there are occasional generalizing couplets of epigrammatic pith:

"The wars you bring to light
Leave their dark in you"

Or

"There are war dead
But no dead wars"

Beyond Repair finishes with a powerful poem called "In Bruges." Here, the lens zoom out, as in Auden's "Musée des beaux arts" which explored the Bruegel's treatment of "human position" of human suffering. Todd assumes an even larger perspective, of time and light, roots and fungi, of "a grieving too particulate to dissipate." If one pays attention, it's still there.

As I type this in Brussels, the war in Ukraine is on everyone's lips. There is another E.U. summit. Journalists are trying to tell us what's happening. It is safe to assume that thoughts and images are being cropped. Now more than ever, like J.C. Todd, we all need to pay attention.

Three Sad Songs of the Maya Woman
Briceida Cuevas Cob
translated by Jonathan Harrington
The Ofi Press, Mexico City, 2020

A RECENT CHAPBOOK in the Contemporary Mexican Poetry Series by the Ofi Press, *Three Sad Songs of the Maya Woman* charts the stages of loss of an indigenous woman grieving for her deceased mother. Arranged in a chronological triptych and addressed directly to the mother, these poems are charged with both affection and regret.

The book begins on a note of disbelief:

> "the woodpecker of your heart
> has ceased its vigorous pecking in the trunk of your
>   chest.
> Je'iiiiiiiiin, je'iiiiiiiiin."

Although I am unable to read the original version of these poems, the translation by Jonathan Harrington is clear, unmannered and quite accessible. The phrase "Je'iiiiiiiiin, je'iiiiiiiiin" remains untranslated and it recurs a number of times in the text, like a chorus. The context suggests that it is a keening sound of pain, and it effectively punctuates the various stages of the speaker's grief.

The second part, entitled "Bringing Her Mother to be Buried," expands beyond the daughter's immediate perspective to include a sense of a place and the routines of everyday life. It is a world of sun, where her mother kept chickens and turkeys, and the speaker anticipates that her mother's sudden absence will be palpable to the animals. The human community, it's worth noting, is evoked in terms which offer no comfort. Certain individuals are called out by name, such Doña Felipa, Doña Anestasia or Doña Lorenza who "poured venom from their mouths / on the name of my mother." The reason for this hostility is not made explicit, but there is no doubting the depth of conflict. Even after her death, there is no sense of remorse. Quite the contrary:

> "Now they dance,
> they laugh,
> they leap and do pirouettes,
> they party and shoot off rockets"

The final section of the triptych, "While Burying Her Mother," returns to a more intimate focus on the relationship between daughter and mother. Much of this section takes the form of an enumeration:

> "Goodbye to your beauty,
> Goodbye to your face,
> Goodbye to the seeds of yours eyes . . ."

The refrain of "goodbye" is repeated in 11 more lines, offering an inventory of her mother's person. Reading it, I was reminded of the end of *King Lear* where, holding his dead daughter the father struggles to come to terms with the ghastly spectacle. "Do you see this? Look on her, look [. . .] Look there, look there!" In this case, the roles of parent and child are reversed, and the speaker refers to her mother as the "child of my eyes."

The availability of Briceida Cuevas Cob's *Three Sad Songs of the Maya Woman* in a lucid translation is a very welcome development. The publisher, the Ofi Press, is based in Mexico City and clearly their Contemporary Mexican Poetry Series deserves a wider audience.

Four from Ukraine

To a backdrop of bombed buildings on a desolate Kharkiv street, cellist Denys Karachevtsev sits alone on a stool playing Bach's Suite No. 5 in C Minor, in a viral video that will pass into history as one of the most moving documents of the tragedy of Putin's barbarous assault on Ukraine. At the time of writing, over 8000 Ukrainian civilians and forces have been killed in the war, among them an unknowable number of potential artists, writers, and musicians. By the end of the war, Putin will have created a lost generation of artists, robbing Ukraine of a potentially fervent chapter in the nation's cultural history, in the same way his cabal of oligarchs and gangsters have robbed the Russian people.

As a homage to Ukraine's vibrant literary history, here are four works of Ukrainian literature in English translation you can read as a form of fundamentally meaningless yet well-intentioned readerly solidarity.

Patriotism ought to involve a continuous act of self-interrogation and the tireless pursuit of national improvement through the examination of history, rather than falling knock-kneed before a flag. This is reflected across the literature of Ukraine, including in Oksana Zabuzhko's *Fieldwork in Ukrainian Sex* (Amazon Crossing, tr. Halyna Hryn). One the most popular Ukrainian novels of the post-independence period is a strident, experimental, and full-fanged onslaught on the country's culture, history, and machismo, narrated by a feminist writer working in America. The prose is constructed in torturously poetic page-long sentences, with frequent shifts from first to second to third person, blurring the line between autofiction and narrative, as the narrator recounts an abusive relationship within a broader Bernhardian canvas combining a cryptic and hilarious onslaught of snark with reflection, comment, and free-association oddness (a chunk of which is lost to this Ukrainely naïve reader). This sort of novel is usually relegated to DIY indie presses with ten subscribers in the UK. In Ukraine, it was on the bestseller list for ten years. Her epic novel *The Museum of Abandoned Secrets* is also available from Amazon Crossing.

Another of the most successful post-1991 novels, Yuri Andrukhovrch's *The Moscoviad* (Spuyten Duyvil, tr. Vitaly Chernetsky), is a hyperactive hoot narrated in the third and first persons by poet Otto Von F., in exile with a clutch of other tormented and eccentric writers in a "literary dormitory" in Moscow. The narrative style is a nonlinear swirl of set-pieces, with satirical riffs on Ukrainian culture and history, surreal digressions and a parodic Russian spy plot that sees the writer persecuted in classic Soviet fashion by being locked in a cage. The author is a co-founder of the Bu-Ba-Bu poetic group, the closest thing to Oulipo in Eastern Europe, and the novel has honorary commonalities, such as the playful multilingual wordplays, the furious commitment to larks and levity above all, and a blithe dismissal of any tedious old narrative scaffolding that the masses have been conditioned to expect. On a self-indulgent note, the "literary dormitory" has much in common with the edifice in my novel *The House of Writers*, the title of which is (coincidentally) mentioned on p.32. Several works by Andrukhovrch are available in English, including the novels *Perverzion* and *Recreation*, and recently the essay collection *My Final Territory*.

Born in Kyiv in 1887, Sigizmund Krzhizhanovsky was a wilfully elusive writer whose works were published posthumously. The collection of seven fantastical stories *Memories of the Future* (NYRB, tr. Joanne Turnbull) shows him as an heir apparent to the similarly Ukraine-born-but-wrote-in-Russian Gogol. Among the bangers here include 'The Bookmark', an early metafictional story about storytellers losing control of their characters, and 'Someone Else's Theme', a sliver of literary satire spiced with a sprinkling of the fantastical, veering opaquely into weird thickets of wtf until it appears the story has become another entirely. 'The Branch Line' and 'Red Snow' are surrealistic dream-narratives with flickers of Bulgakovian magic, and 'The 13th Category of Reason' is irresistible black comedy. The title tale transports the time-machine yarn to Stalinist Russia in an extremely detailed SF yarn that predates the nouveau roman's parodically exact descriptive exactitude. Joanne Turnbull preserves the wordplay and unusual snakiness of his sentences, making this septet an excellent place to begin. NYRB have translated a wondrous heap of his works, including the mordant oddity *Autobiography of a Corpse*.

The anthology *Before the Storm: Soviet Ukrainian Fiction of the 1920s* (Ardis, tr. Yuri Tkacz) features seventeen Ukrainian writers, twelve of whom perished in Russian gulags in the 1930s and 1940s. A vital snapshot of the breadth of Ukrainian literary talent squandered by the tyranny of Stalinism, the stories showcase a range of emerging literary styles opposed to Soviet realism. The longest piece, by Mykola Khvylovy, from his incomplete novel *The Woodcocks*, takes inspiration from the talky epics of Dostoevsky in its exploration of the identity of modern Ukrainian man, in an era when people were free to have thinky confabs about the merits of communism-cum-fascism. There are pastiches of Sherlock Holmes, twitchy and paranoid homages to Gogol, imagistic stories in surreal pastoral moods, stories exploring the opposition to communism in peasant villages, autofictions on the toils of toadying up to the Soviet Union, and several moderately amusing attempts at light comedy. The volume demonstrates the wealth of styles and movements percolating at the time, from the Free Academy of Proletarian Literature (VAPLITE), apolitical futurism, to a form of modernism influenced by Western Europe.

Other notable works in English translation:

- *From Three Worlds: New Writing from Ukraine*—Ed Hogan (ed.)
- *Depeche Mode / The Orphanage*—Serhiy Zhadan
- *Grey Bees*—Andrey Kurkov
- *Wozzeck*—Yurii Izdryk
- *Herstories: An Anthology of New Ukrainian Women Prose Writers*—Michael M. Naydan
- *Dead Souls / Collected Stories*—Nikolai Gogol
- *Sweet Darusya*—Maria Matios
- *The Sarabande of Sara's Band*—Larysa Denysenko
- *The Lost Button*—Irene Rozdobudko
- *Tango of Death*—Yuri Vynnychuk
- *Peltse and Pentameron*—Volodymyr Dibrova

REVIEW | Kurt Luchs

Music Is Everything: Selected Poems of Slavko Mihalić
Translated by Dasha C. Nisula
Exile Editions, 2019

THIS IS THE SECOND volume of Croatian poetry translated by Dasha C. Nisula, following You With Hands More Innocent by Vesna Parun. As well as bringing the distinctive voice of Slavko Mihalić to readers in English, it confirms Nisula as one of the premiere translators of East European verse in our time.

Mihalić (1928–2007) was one of those rare individuals endowed with multiple talents and the drive to indulge them all simultaneously. He was a writer first and foremost, and chiefly a poet, but also a translator, an editor, a musician and an artist. At certain points in his literary career, when his poetry fell afoul of the regime for one reason or another, or one word or another, he supported himself by his art.

The more enduring benefit of his nonliterary talents, though, was how they informed and transformed his writing. He viewed nature with the eyes of a painter and he heard the sonic subtleties of language with the ears of a musician. Not surprisingly, a number of these poems deal with painting. In "Artist's Soliloquy" he writes about the artist as human sponge, who can be infected simply by portraying the world's distress:

> You pass the brush
> over traces of evil.
> Blood is found
> on your hands.

Many more of these poems are about or inspired by music. Bach receives his due ("Coffee Cantata," "Homage to J. S. Bach"), and other composers are mentioned or referred to in passing. However, Mihalić reserves his greatest affection for Mozart in "Eine Kleine Nachtmusik," "Mozart's Magic Coach," "W. A. Mozart" and several others. The final stanza of "Mozart's Magic Coach" is worth quoting in full, as it is where this collection gets its title:

> Because music is everything since music can do
>   everything.
> When music ceases all the magic
> is only a modest craft. As shoeing a horse
> echoes flutes when the blacksmith is Mozart.
> And a jug of wine sings if Mozart's lips
> touch the oboe. Rain begins to glisten, footsteps
> make sense. hills turn azure, streets
> race and curtains are the bare backs of women
> when on its own plays Mozart's piano.

Mihalić might as well be describing himself because, like music and Mozart, he too can do everything. This varied collection, the distillation of a lifetime, contains love poems ("First Love"), landscapes ("In the Snow"), seascapes ("By the Seashore"), poems of war ("Christmas 1991"), and poems that are somehow both metaphysical and lucidly concrete (the brilliantly titled and written "Who I Am and Am I," among many others).

In a world that is forever writhing and mutating, often seemingly for the worse, Mihalić seeks for what is constant and meaningful. He finds it mostly in human love and in beauty, whether natural or manmade. Despite his passion for music, the key to his understanding all this and writing about it so insightfully is silence and inwardness, which he carries with him at all times. The brief poem "Solitude" ends with this line: "I knock on my own door, from the inside."

Although he subscribes to no ideology and no religion other than art and love and nature and his native land, his central credo would appear to be an undefined spiritual yearning, as in the last stanza from "No Matter What That Means":

> Your town can no longer be recognized
> neither in heaven nor on earth, and you must
> continually go toward the light, no matter what
>   that means.

Or, it could be that given where and when he wrote, and the need to say one thing by means of another, the word "light" may stand for hope and optimism. I don't know, and for the reader it may not matter. As in so much fine poetry, the ambiguity, the openness is its own reward.

The Jacques Lacan Foundation
Susan Finlay
Moist Books, March 2022

POSING AS a public-school arriviste, Nicki Smith takes a position at the soi-disant Jacques Lacan Foundation, a repository for fustians with a penchant for weak wordplay and the byzantine theories of the French theorist, second only to Derrida for impish intellectual charlatanry. Posing as posho Lettuce Croydon-Smith, Nicki manoeuvres herself in a world of glamorous grifters and Ivy League sorority queens, in a satirical environs spiritually in sync with the offices of Quink magazine in Alexander Theroux's harsher *Laura Warholic: A Sexual Intellectual*. The novel is a tame comedy of manners, set in a nonspecific realm of fashionable artists and eggheads.

The narrator frequently italicises all the Americanisms in her prose, overlards her vocalisations with like tonnes of *likes*, and sleeps with avant-garde filmmaker Diego as she is put in charge of the French translation of a new Lacan notebook (having massaged her CV with a spurious bilingual brag). As she clashes with the primly-attired Connecticut crème de la crème, her struggle to maintain the con and retain the poise of her idol Kate Moss becomes an increasing schlepp. Finlay's novel is a farcical send-up of the culture of blaggers and carpetbaggers that has become the modus operandi for seemingly every pursuer of power, from influencers to politicians, as their talents for thrusting themselves forward leave the rest of us pining for something better.

The Trees
Percival Everett
Graywolf Press, September 2021

FROM ABSURD COMEDIES (*Glyph, American Desert*), to puckish self-referential novels (*Erasure, Percival Everett by Virgil Russell*), to unique spins on the murder mystery (*I am Not Sidney Poitier, Assumption*) and a raft of other novels and poetry collections, many out of print stretching back to the early 1980s, Everett has been a redoubtable force on the American literary landscape, carving an utterly unique and extravagant body of work that stands with the finest of contemporary fiction. He returns (at the time of writing—his next novel *Dr. No* is coming in November) with a revisionist take on the deep-fried Southern thriller.

When a series of Trumpian hillbillies are murdered in the very racist town of Money, Mississippi—each victim twinned with a mutilated black corpse clutching their severed testicles, a corpse that disappears from the morgue soon after—two beleaguered black detectives are sent to investigate. Through a wise-cracking local waitress, they meet a 106-year-old root doctor who has documented every victim of lynching in the country, stretching back to the 1910s. The victims seem to have one thing in common—a connection to KKK murders of the past. As in several of Everett's works, the plot is incidental to the blistering satire and snark-tastic political comment (consider the lesser-known epistolary smackdown *A History of the African-American People [Proposed] by Strom Thurmond* for another marvellous example).

Poking into the open wound of white supremacy in the rural south in the pre-Biden era, Everett wields his kiln-fresh poker, creating hilariously racist caricatures that capture the blatant racism unleashed with the election of Trumplethinskin. He takes to the thriller with vim, maintaining a brisk pace in short chapters, balancing mordant humour with a venomous critique on America's unsolvable race riddle, a problem sitting dormant since the end of segregation in the south—illustrated in a powerful sequence of the names of the KKK lynching victims. A master of sharp dialogue, punchy and unflinching satire, Everett once more serves up an irresistible novel that performs another necessary scissor-kick to the gut of modern America.

REVIEW | GREG BEM

Boat People
Mayra Santos-Febres
translated by Vanessa Perez-Rosario
Cardboard House Press, 2021

like a tired ache eating at your side
we must plunge into the sea (31)

ORIGINALLY PUBLISHED in 2005, Puerto Rican Mayra Santos-Febre's Spanish-language *Boat People* is now available in English thanks to the keen translation of Vanessa Perez-Rosario. A poetry collection of the ocean, it's enduring as fluid, as transformative as fixed.

It is also a collection of the people who move across the ocean's surface. "how to / reach the sea? and not surrender midway / on the voyage hunting the dream / to eat." (43). Santos-Febres has constructed a collection reflective of life and death upon the water. It is a book containing the storytelling of those who suffer and those who thrive, those who depart and those who arrive.

Boat People is introduced with subtly brutal imagery: "boat people / mangled bodies / onyx shark" (9). Violence and environmental horror are established from the very beginning of the collection in a vision that passes forward the full spectrum of oceanic horror. The constriction of sitting upon water, of the boat people's lives in vast chaos, evokes a fascinating juxtaposition: hopelessness and fatalism meet borderlessness, freedom, and opportunity. Still, the ocean is one of cruelty and incessant obstacle: "scales of flesh fall / verging on the wave's crest / tide after tide morenita / fall / fall / fall" (11) continues the second poem.

Pérez-Rosario provides an ample discussion of the book in her Translator's Note, describing Santos-Febres's poetry as illuminating those who are invisible, identifying life within the margins, and, more specifically, telling the stories of Caribbean people. While the book's tenses feel of the present, of the undocumented migrants of the here and now, Pérez-Rosario astutely highlights that "boat people" is the term for Vietnamese refugees arriving to the United States by boat throughout the American War in Vietnam, and is also the term for "Haitians who risked their lives at sea during the Duvalier dictatorship" in the middle of the last century (75).

in the anonymous city   nourished by tar you
arrive and swear you're in the ocean's deep (55)

Santos-Febres connects the anonymous migration of the individual to the impossibly large collective whole. Abstraction and intimately precise language pushes and pulls the stories themselves into realms of imagination and hallucination.

The fatalism is amplified by a swollen language of stories of unacknowledgment and brutal survival: "identity unquestioned / and one more to the sea / a watery wilderness" (35). The poet calls forth the fragmentation of our discourse, at large, around the subject of migration along the margins, of consideration of refugees. She casts broad strokes and, moments before and moments later, narrow: "undocumented 4 / with a picture of a national hero in the raft / he plunged into the sea" (17). And she considers the relationship of the individual missing an identity; in transit; invisible. To consider their lives and movement when they are unseen, when they are invisible can be felt throughout the book and its title-less segments: "without papers / identities borrowed / floating under forged names" (49).

The book, 73 pages in total, is half the original Spanish and half new translation. It's dense, contains unimaginable layers, and often, like the ocean itself, feels wholly untouchable. In their most quizzical moments, these poems provide arguments, resolutions, and conclusions from the perspective of the boat people: "insatiable the bloodline stretches along its coasts / the sea creates crystals confused with borders / refulgent things on foreign shores" (71).

"it's a question of letting go / let go completely / see yourself become a drop / of fish sweat suddenly / swept up by a seagull" (71). Santo-Febres's direction describes a painful position, incessant doom and horror, and the pressure to let the ocean, metaphorical or literal, guide.

The mesmerizing poetry of Santos-Febres comes to us from a world not far removed from 17 years ago, as the appearances of the migrating public seem to grow across the Mediterranean, the southern border of the United States, and, as I write this, neighbors of Ukraine; the work feels relevant in . Alongside more recent poetry collections investigating migrations of people (see: Desiree C. Bailey's *What Noise Against the Cane?* (2021); Safiya Sinclair's *Cannibal* (2016); Ocean Vuong's *Night Sky with Exit Wounds*; and Caroline Bergvall's *Drift* (2014), Santos-Febres's *Boat People* offers us its own glimpses of the refugees, whose lives are often tenuously presented in news headlines. Parallels can be made to many, and more than once was I reminded of the ghosts within the Mexican desert from Juan Rulfo.

This new release, *Boat People*, has aged well and been given incredible newness. That we may witness it serve as a keystone work within the canon is nothing short of enlivening. But the to receive is to get, a horror experienced by many each day:

> maybe in the ocean's deep there's an excess of everything that suffocates here. (13)

REVIEW | Venetia Welby

Revenge of the Short Story

Reverse Engineering
Scratch Books, March 2022

THE READING PUBLIC loves a short story. Even the novel is getting shorter. Persuading a publisher to go for a collection, though, has been a tough business for many years now. Ideally, the writer will have already sold a few hundred thousand copies of their critically acclaimed four novels before they begin. Failing that, they'll have won a bundle of prizes for those undersized stories they're now waving about: puny, yes, but proven. Investment then, the publisher speculates, may not be thankless. This sclerotic scene is begging for someone to come and crack it open and new publisher Tom Conaghan is your man. Scratch Books is a house that makes the short story king.

In their first book, *Reverse Engineering*, Scratch celebrates the short form by subverting the traditional form of the collection. Seven short stories by well-loved authors such as Irenosen Okojie and Chris Power are followed by forensic interviews with each writer, dissecting the story, the writing process, the hunches, decisions and regrets. The cover indicates a Seventies textbook, and there is certainly a fascinating educational aspect to it, an evaluation of the nuts and bolts of craft that should shore up even the most reluctant writer—but above all, it is a celebration of creativity itself in all its mystery, viewed through the accessible lens of short form fiction. It's such an obviously good idea, that like all such things it makes you wonder why no one's done it before.

The stories have nothing in common except 'the same vivacious diversity', Conaghan acknowledges in the introduction: it is the form of the collection that provides unity and produces something greater than the sum of its parts, each part, however, being uniquely enjoyable. It is a strong first cohort of stories (a second volume will be published later in the year). In 'Mrs Fox' Sarah Hall explores a man's love for his unknowable wife after she is transformed into an even less knowable vixen, all 'nerve and instinct. Her thousand feral programmes'. His attempts to contain her from the wild are futile; when he wraps her up and carries her, 'her brightness escapes the coat at both ends; it is like trying to wrap fire'. He must then, again, recalibrate his identity when his wife bears four wild cubs. 'The Flier' by Joseph O'Neill is similarly magical but lighter hearted: a man who has mysteriously gained the power of flight must contend with the practical implications of doing so in the real world. This superhero power is more of a curse: 'My kind of aerial motion felt like sideways falling: it was scary, slightly nauseating, and unpleasant'. The mundane reactions of others to this miracle leads him into the bureaucratic tangle of trying to get himself insured, and then the story takes an unexpected turn. 'The First Punch' by Jon McGregor is brutally and viscerally rooted in realism. The story cuts back and forth between 'the hot roar of pain' of a man being relentlessly beaten up and the scenario that may have led to this violence: 'the first time she ever touched me . . . suddenly pulling away as though scorched on a hotplate'.`

Conaghan is a skilled interviewer and listening in to his intimate conversations feels almost voyeuristic at times. He knows that, 'Understanding writers' craft is less like a nautical map than learning to read the stars—it's not important knowing the route if the purpose of the voyage is to get lost.' As such, he elicits a respect for the ineffable quality of a story, its own movements and the work of the unconscious. Frequently his authors don't know why, or what they think about a character, an ending, the turn a story demanded it took. 'The widening came out of nowhere,' says Mareen Sohail of her story 'Hair'; 'I didn't see it coming either,' says O'Neill of the change of scene in 'The Flier', and exclaims, 'Their recurring was unconscious!' in response to a question about themes. The power of intuition comes up time and time again: 'I find the voice and *feel* that it works . . . as I write it becomes more of a feeling than a conscious decision,' says Jessie Greengrass. Irenosen Okojie agrees: 'as with most stories, you feel your way through it by instinct.' These days, now The Author has done the whole 'Death of' thing and been violently resuscitated, PRs expect writers to talk slickly about their work and have all the answers—to promote their books. The more uncertain probing of the mysterious nature of writing in *Reverse Engineering* is refreshing and necessary. It is also matched by a great deal of detailed, practical and helpful advice as each element of the story is questioned and unravelled.

It's good to see the short story getting the love it deserves, and being shown to deserve it through deconstruction of its whims and ways. *Reverse Engineering* should act as an instruction manual for some and inspire a publishing revolution in others. The short story's time has come (again).

No, No Duende Here

Leaving the Atocha Station

Ben Lerner

Coffee House Press, August 2011

"The next real literary 'rebels' in this country might well emerge as some weird bunch of anti-rebels . . . who dare somehow to back away from ironic watching, who have the childish gall actually to endorse and instantiate single-entendre principles . . . Who eschew self-consciousness and hip fatigue. [. . .] The new rebels might be artists willing to risk the yawn, the rolled eyes, the cool smile, the nudged ribs, the parody of gifted ironists, the 'Oh how *banal.*' "

—David Foster Wallace, "E Unibus Pluram"

THERE IS GREAT EMPHASIS on the new in our culture. A new product is somehow better *because* it is new, thanks no doubt to our corporate-consumer society. While there's some justification for queuing up to buy the new iPhone or trading in your car every couple of years for the latest model (the Acura XLE pinches you if you nod off at the wheel!), the idea makes less sense when it comes to literature. Any number of classics, after all, are still widely read. And yet the addiction to whatever's stacked on the New Fiction table persists (that's why booksellers have a New Fiction table). The reading public's memory seems to be shrinking, and this literary amnesia, coupled with the conviction that new books are inherently better than old, accounts for the remark, by Pulitzer Prize–winning critic Michael Dirda, that "More books of worth and value are going out of print than are being published today."

And much of the new—relevant, up to date, *modern*—seems to come with a certain amount of irony, cynicism, snark, self-consciousness, self-reference, or some cocktail of two or more of these ingredients served with a whitened smile hovering over a tall glass. Twenty-seven years ago, in his seminal essay "E Unibus Pluram," David Foster Wallace pointed out that "The best TV of the last five years has been about ironic self-reference like no previous species of postmodern art could ever have dreamed of" and that "self-conscious irony" is "the nexus where television and fiction converse and consort."

Arguably, the changing of the guard in literature, from realism to irony-laden fiction and metafiction, began with Pynchon in the '60s. The Vietnam era brought with it widespread distrust, especially of the government, and justified the cynicism that began to pervade the arts. But the disillusionment that followed the hippies' failure to bring about world peace and universal love seems to have apotheosized it.

Even by 1993 the Age of Irony had lasted way too long. Wallace, quoting Lewis Hyde, warns that "Irony has only emergency use." "[I]rony," he explains, "entertaining as it is, serves an almost exclusively negative function. It's critical and destructive, a ground-clearing. [. . .] But it's singularly unuseful when it comes to constructing anything to replace the hypocrisies it debunks." To be merely ironic is to delight in war but not in peace, in demolition—who doesn't secretly fancy swinging a sledgehammer like Thor at defenseless walls?—but not creation.

The ironic attitude toward everything has led, as Wallace warned, to the refusal, in both fiction and society, to take a stance, to be serious, to in any way be—how totally uncool—sincere. Criticism abounds; solutions are passé. Everyone wants to become part of the Party of Can't, offering unchecked mirth to anyone who is so insufferably naïve as to take an interest in a better world.

Enter Ben Lerner and his debut novel, *Leaving the Atocha Station*, a hit with both critics and readers. *The New Statesman*, *The Wall Street Journal*, *Newsweek*, and the *Boston Globe* named it one of the best books of 2011 as did *The Guardian* (UK), the latter calling it "intensely and unusually brilliant." *The New Yorker* included it in its Reviewers' Favorites from 2011. Jonathan Franzen and Paul

Auster enthusiastically blurbed it. It won the 2011 Believer Book Award, and it was a runner-up or finalist for four other prizes. —However cleverly contrived, *Leaving the Atocha Station* nonetheless strikes me as a mediocre book. The fact that so many publications named it one of the best of 2011 seems a measure of how out of touch the literary establishment has become. Alisa Sniderman, writing for *The Last Magazine* (Aug. 27, 2014), ends a piece about Lerner's second novel by referencing a section of Wallace's "E Unibus Pluram," in which Wallace wonders where fiction can go next. "The answer," she proclaims, "is Ben Lerner." And yet his first novel, which is included in her portentous judgment, has broadened and deepened the very trend that, as Wallace warned, has corroded our arts and culture. It is yet another novel that dodges sincerity as though one bite would begin the zombie apocalypse, gives us a main character who is a watcher rather than a doer (and watches himself watching more than anything else), that has mostly substituted referencing other works for creating meaning of its own. So either I inhabit an alternate reality in which Bernie Sanders is president and *Atocha* deserves the praise heaped on it, or the Literary Establishment needs to check its instruments.

I wouldn't begrudge Lerner his accolades or bring up ancient history—2011, after all—except for the literary version on Gresham's law: every mediocre (or outright bad) book published buries every good book one book deeper. I'm thinking of all the people who read *Atocha Station* because it was on "best" and "buzz" lists but will never get to books such as Rilke's *The Notebooks of Malte Laurids Brigge*, Marilynne Robinson's *Housekeeping*, or the two most germane to this essay, William Gaddis's *The Recognitions* and John Berger's *A Painter of Our Time*.

A *Painter of Our Time* was published in 1958, when Cold War temperatures were well below zero. Critics, reacting to the novel's overt socialism and projecting onto it totalitarian sympathies, were all but unanimous in their condemnation. The most prominent, Stephen Spender, went so far as to compare Berger to a young Goebbels. Reeling from this concerted attack, the publisher withdrew the novel. "After one month's life," Berger wrote in 1988, "my first book became a dead letter." (Quite a different reception from the one Lerner's debut novel received.)

A Painter of Our Time recounts the travails of Janos Lavin, a Hungarian painter living in London in the early 1950s, when Hungary is undergoing social and political upheaval. The AVO, Hungary's state police, are arresting, imprisoning, and torturing thousands. Many, like Janos's fellow revolutionary Lazlo, are executed. Others are deported to the hinterlands of the Soviet Union. By 1956, the year the novel ends, Russian tank treads are chewing up the streets of Budapest.

A Painter is a portrait of the aging artist as an émigré. Janos is talented but unknown. A dedicated socialist whose eye is drawn south- and eastward by events in Hungary, he wonders how can he continue to paint—let alone in the safety and calm of England—while his compatriots risk or sacrifice their lives for a cause he believes in just as fervently. The book's title echoes Mikhail Lermontov's *A Hero of Our Time*, quietly reminding us that the artist of conscience hears a call that, to answer, demands he jilt his muse.

In a few brushstrokes Berger contrasts Janos's experiences in Hungary and Germany with his wife's activism in England:

> [Diana] had never been hungry. She had never been interrogated. She had never been smuggled over a frontier. She had sat in committee-rooms. She had shouted in Trafalgar Square. [. . .] She had never been cut-off. Whereas Janos was entirely cut-off. His voice, that had whispered a warning to a companion as he jumped off a tram before his destination to deceive a suspected pursuer, called her Rosie.

Fittingly enough (in the context of this essay), Janos's work doesn't sell because it's perceived as old-fashioned. "He clearly has talent," admits a gallery owner. "But it's work, don't you know, that very much belongs to the twenties and thirties."

ADAM GORDON is very different from Berger's protagonist. A privileged young poet who gets a year of study in Madrid courtesy of a handsome fellowship, he can't claim even Diana's level of social involvement. Adam scores the free money by proposing an epic-length poem backgrounded by the Spanish Civil War. The only problem is he knows nothing—nor does he care to know anything—about the war, Spanish history, or even Spanish poetry. He's a slacker who spends his days smoking hash, loitering in the Prado, ignoring his faux epic, and orchestrating complex facial expressions and subtle tones of voice in order to mislead everyone around him about what he actually thinks and feels. He has mastered what Wallace calls the "game of appearance poker." Adam is also fond of admitting he is a "fraud" and fretting aloud that he is "pretending" to be a poet.

The book opens in the poet's attic apartment (Chatterton anyone?). We follow him as he walks around Madrid like the Hollywood clone of an alienated, angst-ridden artist who has little social life and no real friends. Shallow, unlikeable, and pathologically self-absorbed, he's obsessed with the impression he makes on everyone around him. His dread is so pronounced he feels "threatened by" people in a club who, possessed by the loa of music, are oblivious to how they might look to others.

It should come as no surprise that someone so taken with surfaces spends the whole novel dithering around articulating something meaningful without ever quite getting around to it. Oh he *references* various concepts, as when he wonders "if the incommensurability of language and experience was new," but aside from the fact that this particular incommensurability predates the fall of Rome, he will never get more than ankle-deep into anything. Ironically, we are expected to lend credence to someone who spends most of his time *evading* life—avoiding actual relationships and authentic communication—when he offers vague perceptions of a deeper dimension to reality. And why does someone so obsessed with appearances *care* what's underneath? Lerner never bothers to reconcile these opposing tendencies.

As part of his schtick, Adam spends a lot of time denying art can inspire a "profound experience," that poetry is worth committing to paper or worth reading, and that *anyone* is genuine. Possibly, we're not supposed to believe Adam's bald statements about art. At one point, for example, he's on the verge of being transported out of his narcissistic bubble by a song sung in Portuguese, so perhaps he *is* capable of a profound experience of art after all. He has also made a morning ritual of going to El Prado and planting himself in front of a Van der Weyden painting. Senses altered by hash and coffee, he could be after the profound experience of art he dismisses. Then again, these museum trips could represent his repeated (and unsuccessful) attempts to be moved by Van der Weyden's masterpiece. Whatever the case, Lerner seems to have gotten so involved in constructing a labyrinth he forgot to put a minotaur in it, and the reader merely gets lost in layers of double meanings and uncertainties. Instead of leading us somewhere, Adam is like Wallace's "well-conditioned TV viewer," and the "most frightening prospect" he faces is leaving himself "open to others' ridicule by betraying passé expressions of value, emotion, or vulnerability." Adam does, however, *fake* vulnerability as when he claims his "brilliant and uwaveringly supportive mother" is dead. Lerner passes this off as humor.

To avoid betraying passé expressions of value, Adam likes to blurt out parodies of academicese, such as when Isabel asks why Americans are studying Franco instead of Bush. "The proper names of leaders," Adam replies, "are distractions from concrete economic modes." Lerner does something similar when a group of Spaniards are discussing a poetry reading in which Adam participated; the Spaniards are portrayed pretentious dupes who utter aesthetic pseudo-profundities.

While poetry may be, as Adam implies, basically useless, while it may be true that poems are never "machines that could make things happen," the accusations have a false ring coming from him: Adam never has to make a choice between writing poetry and fighting for a cause. His life consists of rolling "spliffs," wandering around Madrid high, and wasting his fellowship.

Berger's protagonist, on the other hand, is tormented throughout the novel by his decision to paint rather than take part in leftist agitation until he finally abandons his passion (something Adam lacks in any form), rejoins the fight for class equality, and sacrifices what he has so long sought: critical acclaim and a modicum of commercial success. After Janos sends a single letter from Hungary, his voice goes silent: he's either been killed or thrown into prison. Adam, in chiaroscuro-like contrast, neither risks nor sacrifices anything. His big decisions generally revolve around how to arrange his face or affect a tone of voice.

Admittedly, *Atocha* is a send-up—one that occasionally breaks into seriousness—so it's hard to tell whether Adam means what he says he means when he says he really means it. (The use of photographs in the novel, spoofing W.G. Sebald, is one reminder among many the book is a send-up.) But reviewers seem to be in denial about *how much* of the book is cheeky fluff. James Wood, writing for *The New Yorker*, suggests that the cheap humor and eye-rolling jokes are an insignificant part of *Atocha*. He also warns us not to characterize the book "only in negative terms—by what it refuses or mocks or evades." But why shouldn't we when what the book primarily does is refuse, mock, and evade?

Take the drowning witnessed by two Americans traveling in Mexico and imported by Adam via email. "The real" is referenced in such a cliché way—death makes an experience more "real" (the emailer himself puts "real" in quotes)—that Adam is compelled to point out how cliché it is. To make the scene more metafictiony, one of the two American friends is writing a novel and, as her boyfriend observes, gets "some good material for her novel." No one explains why a drowning in a Mexican river is "good material" for a novel, but Adam is envious because his friends are having a "real" experience "not just the experience of experience sponsored by" a fellowship. It doesn't occur to him that no one forced him to spend his days spliffing, holed up with Cervantes and Tolstoy, wandering Madrid throwing face fakes at everyone.

The real evasion comes when Adam chances on a death scene of his own: "I arrived at what they call a scene of mayhem. It was cloudy. There were police and medical workers and other people everywhere, many of them weeping and/or screaming, and, as I got closer to the station, more and more confusion." Lerner actually devotes far more verbiage to the emailed drowning than to the bombing. Nor is there any attempt to render the aftermath of the bombing in real time or to reflect any sort of urgency. Instead, he proffers "what they call scene of mayhem," a stock phrase of calculated distance. And then there's the use of *and/or*, a term more befitting a legal contract, which signals Adam's aloofness: where would his façade of world weariness be if he made an effort to actually convey the horror of this grisly incident?

A T FIRST GLANCE it's easy to mistake Adam for Lerner's alter ego: both are poets, hail from Kansas, and spent a year in Madrid on fellowship. But these are incidentals. Adam Gordon is probably closer to the protagonist of David Foster Wallace's short story "Good Old Neon," with a dash of Otto Pivener (from Gaddis's *The Recognitions*) thrown in.

"Good Old Neon," narrated by the ghost of a yuppie named Neal, begins: "My whole life I've been a fraud." Neal's subsequent self-analysis could hardly do a better job of describing Adam: "I seemed to be so totally self-centered and fraudulent that I experienced everything in terms of how it affected people's view of me and what I needed to do to create the impression of me I wanted them to have." Equally apt: ". . . I'd somehow chosen to cast my lot with my life's drama's supposed audience instead of with the drama itself, and . . . even now was watching and gauging my supposed performance's quality and probable effects . . ."

Neal boils his problem down to his being a yuppie incapable of love (and hates how cliché that sounds). Although Adam's stated problem is that he "was incapable of a profound experience of art" (which must be particularly rough on a supposed poet), he shows no depth of feeling for anyone. His romantic interests, Isabel and Teresa, are important to him only has they reflect a gratifying image of himself. While Neal and Adam's fraudulence and inability to emote are the key players in their shared identity, there's a pretty good supporting cast.

Neal throws out this line: "I was a fair-haired boy and on the fast track but wasn't happy at all, whatever happy means . . ." Wallace uses the same "whatever" construction again five pages later. Adam turns this into a verbal tic: ". . . I didn't have to worry about building a community, whatever that meant . . . "; ". . . the swifts, if that's what they were . . ."; ". . . what kind of grown man, if that's what he was . . ."; ". . . reading poetry, if that is even the word . . ."; "nothing was more American, whatever that means, than fleeing the American, whatever that is . . .", etc. The examples go well into double digits.

Another odd similarity hinges on how Neal talks about the one woman he thinks he might have loved: "And I never really saw her, I couldn't see anything except who I might be in her eyes." Lerner gives this a twist and turns it into parody: ". . . I found myself avoiding her eyes, because when I looked at or into them, I believed I saw she saw right through me. Or I saw her see herself reflected in my eyes, saw that she knew or was coming to know, that what interest I held for her was virtual, that my appeal for her had little to do with my actual writing or speech . . ."

Neal and Adam also immolate many mental calories wondering about the limitations of language, Neal in an earnest—even pained—way, Adam in a way that is mostly smokescreen, that is, in ways too general or trite to be genuine.

A parallel here or there between Neal and Adam would undoubtedly be accidental, but the key points of congruence—and their specificity—suggest something more deliberate.

Adam's other literary antecedent is Otto Pivener, the poseur from *The Recognitions*, Gaddis's 956-page tome, which abounds in counterfeiters, fakes, and frauds. Jonathan Franzen described the novel as "an ur-text of postwar fiction, both the granddaddy of difficulty and the first great cultural critique, which, even if Heller and Pynchon hadn't read it while composing *Catch-22* and *V.*, managed to anticipate the spirit of both." And yet upon its publication in 1955, *The Recognitions* was almost universally panned by critics, many of whom, it would later turn out, had never actually read the book, and Gaddis was driven into an exile from which he would not emerge for two decades.

One of Otto's outstanding features is his habit of taking other people's experiences or words and relating them as if they are his own. Time and again his fakery is ruthlessly (and hilariously) exposed. At one point Otto sojourns in a South American country where he finishes a play he's been working on. A revolution erupts, and although he's nowhere near the fighting, he puts an arm in a sling. Once back in New York, he angles conversations toward the insurrection, implying he was injured while escaping the violence. Adam uses the email from Latin America in the same way. He recounts to Isabel the story of the drowning in Mexico, except that he places himself and a former girlfriend in the story. He also parrots things other people say, offering them, as does Otto, as his own. The name of Otto's alter ego—that is, the hero of his play—is Adam's surname: Gordon. Possibly coincidence but, in a novel so awash in literary allusions, probably not.

This tracing out of Adam Gordon's template isn't to suggest Lerner merely lifted him from the pages of other authors—there's plenty about Adam that's autobiographical, among other things—nor is it intended to be accusatory; one source for a character is probably as valid as another. Rather, I think it's useful to see how Adam differs from Neal and Otto and how differently things work out for him.

The Recognitions asks what is authentic in American society. *A Painter of Our Time* asks what is most worth our time—on what do we spend our human capital? The question *Atocha* asks is: What happens if a fraud like Adam, who isn't much bothered by his fraudulence, isn't exposed and things work out for him? The answer is the novel's ending: a showy launch for a bilingual chapbook of Adam's poetry. Pretty much everyone he's mentioned in the novel shows up, and, having fooled his audience, Adam feels fulfilled. He is delighted to admire himself being admired (in stark contrast to Neal, whose existential emptiness drives him to suicide). The final line of *Atocha*, "Then I planned to live forever in a skylit room surrounded by my friends," is slightly updated version of "And he lived happily ever after." The novel is comedy, without the laughs.

WHEN I MENTION *A Painter of Our Time*, I find most literati haven't even heard of it, let alone read it. Nonetheless, it's still available as a handsome Vintage paperback. *The Recognitions* was a Penguin Twentieth Century Classics edition until Penguin quietly let it go. It was rescued from oblivion by Dalkey Archive Press, which then surrendered the rights to New York Review Books Classics. While these two landmark novels, which had difficult births and inspiring revivals, may no longer be "trending," they have stayed in print for well over half a century—no mean feat.

So perhaps the new replacing the old is not inevitable. Perhaps they can exist, side by side. But it is too much to ask that *comparable* books enjoy each other's company?

Leaving the Atocha Station, for all its hinting at the metaphysical conundrums embedded in things like language, never delivers anything substantive. Ultimately it is surface shine, like the gleam off El Estanque, a man-made lake in Madrid central to Adam's reveries. In one meditation he frets over the shortcomings of his poetry, concluding there's "no duende here," an appraisal that is, perhaps, more fitting than he realizes.

In the end, whether or not someone likes a book is largely a function of taste, and mine is no better than anyone else's. Time, I suppose, will ultimately sort out whether it's I or the literary establishment who's misjudged *Leaving the Atocha Station*. Some things, however, are not a matter of preference. It's astonishing, for example, that although Wallace states unequivocally that dispensing with "ironic watching," "self-consciousness," and "hip fatigue" while getting behind "single-entendre principles" might be the smelling salts that snap fiction out of its torpor, critics like Alisa Sniderman think Lerner is just what Dr. Wallace prescribed.

In *A Painter of Our Time*, Janos says the skill painters "need and acquire so slowly" can be equated to a trick—the trick of accomplished technique. He contrasts this with the more common notion of a trick, which is a "copied mannerism," a gimmick. The latter, he says, tries to get the better of the picture: "you are playing a trick on yourself, deceiving yourself, pretending you have more feeling, more skill, more experience than you actually have, and in the other case you are trying to get the better of your subject, of reality. Getting the better of the real—is to be an artist." I cannot convince myself it's the real Lerner has gotten the better of.

Genesis 0
Isabelle Nicou
Translated by Katie Shireen Assef
Amphetamine Sulphate, 2021
Originally published as *Genèse 0* by Éditions de
la Différence, Paris, 2007

T HERE IS A STORY in 90s rock lore of Donita Sparks, lead singer and guitarist of all-female grunge-rock group L7 removing and throwing her (bloody, naturally) tampon out into the crowd at the 1992 Reading festival. While a 2020 Guardian article has it that the incident was a response to crowd heckling, back in 1993 Spin magazine did not offer context, merely referring to it as a 'punk breakthrough'. If it was equitable with—if not out-performing—men's antics in the dick-swinging business of music back then, it was also a contrast to another kind of grunge female, that of the stylised 'kinderwhore' of Courtney Love with ripped vintage dresses and smudged makeup.

Regardless of the reasons why the tampon went down in pop-culture history, it remains memorable for something more important but overlooked in its simplicity. It was a moment of supremely ugly reality which at the same time was perfectly mundane if you were a woman who'd experienced a period; a reality of being female for many that was somehow a lot more shocking in its banality than anything Courtney did, or her precursor in performance, Wendy O. Williams.

No matter the labelling: ugly, mundane, or even surreal, it also sums up the divide in a certain kind of women's writing. Whether fictional, autobiographical, or anything that falls in between, and despite the homogenous praise of 'urgent' and 'powerful' that tends to gets paraded any time a woman writer delves into what can be seen as squeamish issues: sexual trauma, desire, abortion, the sense is that a writer's intimacies are to an extent being stylised for mass consumption hovers above the page. While the mere writing of such subjects is deemed praiseworthy, there is still little in the way of actual criticism that asks for more thorough thinking in them: the internal hows and whys rather than just emotive set-pieces. In terms of the L7 incident, women's writing wants to know we bleed (unproblematically), but doesn't want to see the tampon, much less us taking it out.

It's impossible to know exactly why or how this happens. To speculate, most likely it is a combination of a conscious or unconscious self-censorship—understandable if you decide to go down the road of that genre—and judicious editing with an eye for sales and the all-important female 're-latability', with a lack of acknowledgement that too much thinking on the page does not equal sales in terms of books aiming to get on bestseller lists. Ottessa Moshfegh's ultra-graphic descriptions of bodily functions inspire both disgust and praise as well as sales, but the author is also something of a rarity in that she at least appears superficially to not give a shit, or revels in the performance of pretending so.

But the swing from glossy to almost gleefully graphic asks the question, where is the everyday ugly real in women's writing: the kind that neither relies on redemptive, simplistic narrative or provocation? The answer can in part be found in French author Isabelle Nicou's *Genesis 0* (tr. Katie Shireen Assef). Published by Amphetamine Sulphate, it is simply a story of a woman's pregnancy and abortion. Its brevity (only 107 pages) serves to amplify the unsentimental internal monologue of its protagonist, Elizabeth, as she goes about her daily life. An actress by profession, but acting outside of it, her new growth is a secret that removes her from herself in the way a character would: 'neither my words nor my gestures belong to me.'

Elizabeth's detached observations of the foetus, her life, and memories clash in both grotesque and philosophical streams of consciousness. This is extreme flux without literary histrionics, a mind in communication with a physical intrusion. Her thoughts move from the divine to the cannibalistic: not out of hatred but a kind of darkly humorous anti-love which could be said to be a form of endearment, one that recognises possibility whilst acknowledging she is ultimately the destructor. 'You the thing' is merely a form that will never achieve externality, and so Elizabeth, as its temporary carrier, allows the essence to shape itself through her thoughts in sanguine symbiosis.

Genesis 0 is an 'I' story devoid of any attachment to itself at a time where the 'I' is derided, perhaps not unfairly, due to its shift from telling a story with a personal aspect within a greater context to expanding its meaning to be the 'I' as both earth and sun. It is true that there is just Elizabeth, the thing, and her consciousness, and yet all three feel transient: replaceable, interchangeable. If the thing is faceless and formless in the sense of the external, so too, is Elizabeth, the actor's pliability suggesting other characters for her unconscious:

> 'I'm the one you chose (you the thing). But it's Joan of Arc that I should be playing. Voices. Voices and nothing else. How proud mom would be of me if she knew! I'm the sole repository of meaning, the only one to understand the fatality that whispers here or there, at all hours of the day.'

There is a joke embedded in the fact that Elizabeth is playing Aricia in a production of Racine's *Phèdre*; in the *Aeneid*, Aricia is a divine place associated with childbirth—and her relationship with the actor playing Hippolytus. Her outer and inner lives in such a combination take on the feeling not of a Moebius strip—upon discovering that the thing will not leave as carefully planned—but a Klein bottle, where there is no exit and the boundaries of self become constricting where they once appeared liberating.

In an interview with Amphetamine Sulphate on Dennis Cooper's site, Nicou confirms the ideas of both the mundane ugly real and the ultra-'I' that still manages detachment: 'The narrative, as strong as it is, is also extremely common: a woman having a breakup or an abortion, you find these elements in a lot of novels. What is really important to me is how deep the "I" can get, how the first-person writing permeates the reader, how an "I" supplants another . . . In fact, reading, as I practice it and as I would like to induce it, is an experience of mental alienation.'

Nicou's 'I' is one that has less in common with the 'I' of more mainstream women's writing, and more with that of the 'I' of Hélène Cixous where the focus of the self is in stream of consciousness reflection and exploration rather than that of laying out a simplistic join-the-dots narrative. In a *Los Angeles Review of Books* essay of 2015, Benjamin Crockett notes that 'Cixous offers a way of writing that will allow women to "transform their history, to seize the occasion to speak." She declares, "[n]early the entire history of writing is confounded with the history of reason [. . .] it has been one with the phallocentric tradition."'

The underlying reasoning that fuels the narrative of *Genesis 0*, that Elizabeth will have a straightforward abortion by pill, is thwarted, and against this complication, plunges her into more internality to the point where she exists almost solely inside herself; alongside the thing, divinity and motherhood co-existing with destruction. It is hard to envision the core demographic (as publishers imagine them) of books such as *Three Women* or *My Year of Rest and Relaxation* being able to grasp *Genesis 0*—though of course one hopes that is not the case. Without flashily displaying its intellect, it is a book that is nevertheless steeped in thought, the kind that refracts the myriad of states one goes through—sometimes at the same time—in such a situation: anxiety, humour, despair. Its graphic moments and looping, wild streams of consciousness are not there for the sake of shock and derangement. Instead, they are a long consideration of the connection between women's bodies, minds, and the internal conversations that spring from them, waiting to emerge into the greater world.

Caleb Nichols

DEATH OF A CLAM

The gull hovers, drops
its catch from about 30 feet.
It's hard for me to imagine that

doing the trick—that even dropped
from that height, the sand
wouldn't break its fall,

wouldn't keep its shell intact.
It almost seems like the sand
should swallow the clam, hide it

once it again at least from the gulls,
if not the sickled beaks
of the curlews on the beach,

the birds we used to näively
call *sandpipers* because
of the way they'd pipe crabs down,

& also because of their call. Sandpipers,
though, are so much closer
to plovers—small, skittish,

a bird that could bathe in an open shell
but would stand no chance
at breaking in to the creature

inside. I've read that clams
have no sentience, or at least no brain,
and so are morally acceptable,

as animals, to eat. Thank goodness, too—
what a horrible death! Being
drug out of bed in the beak

of the reaper, and dropped
from such great heights.

Contributors

Iván **Arguëlles** is an innovative and prolific Mexican-American poet. The author of some fifty collections, he has received the William Carlos Williams Award, the American Book Award, and a Lifetime Achievement Award from the Before Columbus Foundation. His recent collection, *The Blank Page*, was published by Sagging Meniscus in 2021.

Pablo Baler is Professor of Latin American Literature and Creative Writing at California State University, Los Angeles and International Research Fellow at The Center for Fine Art Research at Birmingham City University, U.K. Among other titles, Baler is the author of the award winning novel *Circa* (1999), the essay *Latin American Neo Baroque: Senses of Distortion* (2008, 2016) and the novel *Chabrancán* (2020).

Greg Bem is a poet and librarian in Seattle.

Russell Bennetts is a poet and economist. *Berfrois the Book* was published by Dostoyevsky Wannabe in 2019. *Go Ovenbaked*, with Judson Hamilton and Colin Raff, was published by Pendant Publishing in the very same year.

Chwen-Yuen Angie Chen is an internal and addiction medicine physician at an academic institution running a busy integrated primary care chemical dependency service. She has co-authored peer-reviewed medical journal articles and textbook chapters on substance use disorders and physician suicide. Before medicine, she was a film maker trained at NYU and a Tibetan Buddhist Nun who was ordained in Kathmandu. She's a golf mom and avid longboard surfer. Her professional work has appeared in *Frontiers in Medicine*, *Global Psychiatry*, *Journal of General Internal Medicine*, as well as textbook chapters in *Lifestyle Medicine Handbook*, *The Art and Science of Physician Wellbeing*, and *Connect Core Concepts in Health*. Her "Six-Word-Memoir" was also chosen for the COVID pandemic issue, *A Terrible, Horrible, No Good Year*.

Marvin Cohen is the author of many novels, plays, and collections of essays, stories, and poems. He lives on the Lower East Side of Manhattan.

Elizabeth Cooperman is author (with Thomas Walton) of *The Last Mosaic* (Sagging Meniscus, 2017) and co-editor (with David Shields) of the anthology *Life Is Short—Art is Shorter* (Hawthorne Books, 2014). Her work has appeared in *Writer's Chronicle*, *Seattle Review*, *1913: A Journal of Forms*, and elsewhere.

Vincent Czyz's essays and articles have appeared in *New England Review*, *Boston Review*, *AGNI*, *West Branch*, *Longreads*, *Poets & Writers*, *Rain Taxi*, *The Arts Fuse*, *Translation Review*, and *New Millennium Writings*, among other venues. The author of a fiction collection, a novel, and a novella, he is the recipient of several fellowships and awards. His short stories have been printed in publications such as *Shenandoah*, *AGNI*, *The Massachusetts Review*, *Copper Nickel*, *Tampa Review*, *Tin House*, and *Georgetown Review*.

Bradley David's poetry and prose appears in *Plainsongs*, *SEISMA*, *Porridge Magazine*, *Stone of Madness*, *Epoch Press*, and *Spuyten Duyvil Dispatches Editions*. New work is forthcoming in *Fruit Journal*, *Milk & Cake Press*, and *Torrey House Press*.

Jack Foley's numerous books of poetry, fiction and criticism include *Visions and Affiliations*, a "chronoencyclopedia" of California poetry from 1940 to 2005, *Grief Songs* (Sagging Meniscus, 2017) and *When Sleep Comes* (SM, 2020). He lives in Oakland and hosts a weekly radio show, *Cover to Cover*, on Berkeley's Pacifica station, KPFA.

Jake Goldsmith, 24, is a writer with cystic fibrosis and the founder of The Barbellion Prize, a book prize for ill and disabled authors. He is the author of a memoir, *Neither Weak Nor Obtuse* (SM, 2022).

John Patrick Higgins is a playwright, short story writer, screenwriter and director. He lives in Belfast.

Tomoé Hill's work has appeared in such publications as *Socrates on the Beach*, *The London Magazine*, *Vol. 1 Brooklyn*, *3:AM Magazine*, *Music & Literature*, *Numéro Cinq*, and *Lapsus Lima*, as well as the anthologies *We'll Never Have Paris* (Repeater Books), *Azimuth* (Sonic Art Research Unit at Oxford Brookes University), and *Trauma: Essays on Art and Mental Health* (Dodo Ink).

Charles Holdefer is an American writer currently based in Brussels. His stories have appeared in the *New England Review*, *Chicago Quarterly Review* and *Slice*. His latest novel is *Don't Look at Me* (SM, October 2022).

Nate Logan is the author of *Apricot* (above/ground press, 2022) and *Small Town* (The Magnificent Field,

2021). He's a Visiting Assistant Professor of English at Marian University.

Kurt Luchs is the author of *Falling in the Direction of Up* (SM, 2020), *One of These Things Is Not Like the Other* (Finishing Line Press, 2019), and the humor collection *It's Funny Until Someone Loses an Eye (Then It's Really Funny)* (SM, 2017). He lives in Michigan.

Nora Mapp is a writer and visual artist. She has a BFA from The School of the Art Institute of Chicago and an MFA from Bard College.

Kathleen Nicholls is an author and illustrator, best known for *Go Your Crohn Way*, the first of three books loosely based on her own experiences with chronic illness. She lives and works in central Scotland.

M.J. Nicholls is the author of the novels *Condemned to Cymru* (SM, 2022), *Trimming England* (SM, 2021), *Scotland Before the Bomb* (SM, 2019), The *1002nd Book to Read Before You Die* (SM, 2018), *The Quiddity of Delusion* (SM, 2017), *The House of Writers* (SM, 2016), and *A Postmodern Belch* (2014). He lives in Glasgow.

Caleb Nichols' poetry has been featured in *Hoax, Redivider, DEAR Poetry Journal*, and other places. His chapbook *Teems///\\\Recedes* is forthcoming from Kelp Books. A PhD candidate in Creative Writing at Bangor University in Wales, he is the founder of the SLO Book Bike, a queer-owned, bike-powered, pop-up bookshop in San Luis Obispo, CA.

Bobby Parrott was obviously placed on this planet in error. In his own words, "The intentions of trees are a form of loneliness we climb like a ladder." His poems appear or are forthcoming in *Spoon River Poetry Review, RHINO Poetry, Atticus Review, The Hopper, Poetic Sun, Clade Song, Rabid Oak*, and elsewhere. He currently finds himself immersed in a forest-spun jacket of toy dirigibles, dreaming himself out of formlessness in the chartreuse meditation capsule called Fort Collins, Colorado where he lives with his houseplant Zebrina and his wind-up robot Nordstrom.

Paolo Pergola is the author of *Passaggi—avventure di un autostoppista* (Rides: The Adventures of a Hitchhiker) (Exorma, 2013), *Attraverso la finestra di Snell* (Through Snell's Window) (Italo Svevo Edizione, 2019), and *Reset* (SM, 2021). His work has appeared in several Italian literary magazines. He is a member of OPLEPO/ Opificio di Letteratura Potenziale (Workshop of Potential Literature), Italy's equivalent of France's OULIPO. He lives in Tuscany and works as a zoologist.

C.D. Rose is the author of *The Blind Accordionist* (Melville House, 2021), the final part of a loose parafictional trilogy. 'Drone/Echo' is from the forthcoming work *We Live Here Now*.

Ryan Ruby is a writer and translator from Los Angeles, California. His fiction and criticism have appeared in *The New York Review of Books, The Paris Review Daily, Conjunctions, n+1, The Baffler*, and elsewhere. His debut novel *The Zero and the One* was published in March 2017 by Twelve Books. He is the author of a book-length poem, *Context Collapse*, which was a Finalist for the 2020 National Poetry Series and a Semi-Finalist for the 2020 Tomaž Šalamun Prize. He has translated Roger Caillois and Grégoire Bouillier from the French for Readux Books. A graduate of Columbia University and the University of Chicago, he lives in Berlin, where he is on the faculty of the Berlin Writers' Workshop and an Affiliate Fellow of the Institute for Cultural Inquiry. In 2019, he was the recipient of the Albert Einstein Fellowship from the Einstein Forum in Potsdam.

Mike Silverton is the author of *Anvil on a Shoestring* (SM, 2022). His poetry appeared in the late 60s and early 70s in *Harper's, The Nation, Wormwood Review, Poetry Now, some/thing, Chelsea, Prairie Schooner, Elephant* and elsewhere. William Cole included Mike's poems in four anthologies: *Eight Lines and Under* (Macmillan, 1967), *Pith and Vinegar* (Simon and Schuster, 1969), *Poetry Brief* (Macmillan, 1971), and *Poems One Line & Longer* (Grossman, 1973).

J.A. Tyler is the author of *The Zoo, a Going* (Dzanc Books). His fiction has appeared in *Diagram, Black Warrior Review, Fairy Tale Review, Fourteen Hills, New York Tyrant*, and others..

Thomas Walton is the author of *Good Morning Bonecrusher!* (Spuyten Duyvil, 2021), *All the Useless Things Are Mine* (SM, 2020), *The World Is All That Does Befall Us* (Ravenna Press, 2019), and, with Elizabeth Cooperman, *The Last Mosaic* (SM, 2018). He lives in Seattle.

Venetia Welby, a writer and journalist who lives in London, is the author of the novel *Mother of Darkness* (Quartet, 2017) and the forthcoming *Dreamtime* (Salt, Sept. 2021). Her essays and short fiction have appeared in *The Spectator, The London Magazine, Review 31* and anthologies *Garden Among Fires* and *Trauma*, among others.

www.ingramcontent.com/pod-product-compliance
Lightning Source LLC
Chambersburg PA
CBHW080252280626
47159CB00020B/3452